SCHOLASTIC INC.

Originally published in 2016 in the United Kingdom by
Macmillan Children's Books, an imprint of Pan Macmillan

The characters and events portrayed in this book are fictitious or are used
fictitiously. Any similarity to real persons, living or dead, is purely coincidental
and not intended by the author.

No part of this publication may be reproduced, stored in a retrieval system,
or transmitted in any form or by any means, electronic, mechanical,
photocopying, recording, or otherwise, without written permission
of the publisher. For information regarding permission, write to
Sourcebooks Jabberwocky, an imprint of Sourcebooks, Inc.,
1935 Brookdale Rd., Naperville, IL 60563.

ISBN 978-1-338-23063-5

Copyright © 2016 by Tom Percival. Cover and internal design © 2017
by Sourcebooks, Inc. Text and illustrations © by Tom Percival. All rights
reserved. Published by Scholastic Inc., 557 Broadway, New York, NY 10012,
by arrangement with Sourcebooks Jabberwocky, an imprint of Sourcebooks, Inc.
SCHOLASTIC and associated logos are trademarks and/or registered
trademarks of Scholastic Inc.

The publisher does not have any control over and does not assume any
responsibility for author or third-party websites or their content.

12 11 10 9 8 7 6 5 4 3 2 1   17 18 19 20 21 22

Printed in the U.S.A.   40

First Scholastic printing, October 2017

This book is dedicated to Gastrells School and everyone in it, for being generally AWESOME!

Contents

1. Trimming the Story Tree — 1
2. A Pale Imitation — 13
3. A Sheep in Wolf's Clothing — 25
4. The Green Man's Lair — 35
5. Body Snatcher — 53
6. Role Reversal — 63
7. Be Your Own Wolf — 79
8. The Instruction Manual — 89
9. A Comedy of Errors — 101
10. Through the Looking Glass — 117
11. The Dilemma — 135
12. The Awakening — 143
13. The Truth Comes Out — 151
14. The Secret Garden — 165

I
Trimming the Story Tree

It was the annual trimming of the Story Tree, and *everyone* in Tale Town was excited. Even Sleeping Beauty was excited, and she wasn't even awake, but she *looked* excited— sort of. The Story Tree was the reason the town had first gotten its name. Every one of its many leaves contained a different story. To "read" them, all you had to do was run your finger along the leaf, and that story would happen *inside your head*.

With every new story that was told nearby, a new branch or shoot would sprout on the tree, so it could easily get very overgrown. That is why every year the oldest stories were trimmed from the tree, dried out, and turned into scrolls that were kept in a vault deep beneath the Tale Town library.

Huge crowds had gathered to watch the ceremony, and Jack and Betsy—his magical talking hen—struggled to push their way to the front to meet their friends.

"Excuse me!" called out Jack as he elbowed his way past three little pigs

and three much larger bears. "Coming through!"

"PaaaAaArdon!" squawked Betsy as she hopped up and down in front of Jack.

"Sorry?" said Jack. "What was that, Betsy?"

Betsy rolled her eyes. The only word she'd ever been able to say was *what*, but somehow Jack always knew what she meant. Recently, he'd been trying to teach her some more polite words, like "pardon," but it wasn't really working out.

"WHAaAaaaAaaat!" shrieked Betsy crossly.

"Oh! I see…" said Jack. "You're right. That is Sausage-Face Fitch, but you shouldn't call him that. Mayor Fitch would go crazy if he heard you! Come on. The ceremony's about to begin!"

"Hey, Jack—"

"—there you are!" said Hansel and Gretel as Jack finally got to the front of the crowd. The twins were close—*very* close. Sometimes they could have whole conversations just by waggling their eyebrows at each other.

"Hi, everyone!" called Jack, waving at his friends. Hansel, Gretel, Red, and Anansi all waved back. "Have I missed anything?" he added.

"Not really, but—"

"—Mayor Fitch is *still*—"

"—doing his speech!" replied Hansel and Gretel.

The mayor was standing behind a podium, his shiny, pink face gleaming in the sunlight. He lifted up the ancient stone tablet that the poem "Live Long the Story Tree" was carved into. *Everyone* in Tale Town knew the poem, which had been carved into the stone for almost as long as the town had been there:

LONG AGO, UPON THIS SPOT THE
STORY TREE WAS BORN,

AND WITH IT GREW UP TALE TOWN,
A ROSE WITHOUT A THORN.

BEWARE THE SHADOWS LURKING IN
THE DARKNESS OF THE NIGHT,

WHO WANT TO TAKE AWAY THIS
GIFT AND HIDE FROM US ITS LIGHT.

FOR IF THIS TREE IS DAMAGED THEN
EXPECT THE UNEXPECTED,

THE STORY TREE IS SACRED AND
MUST ALWAYS BE PROTECTED.

LIVE LONG THE STORY TREE!

Anansi scowled while two grumpy-looking spiders, perched on each of his shoulders, clacked their legs together crossly. Some people are afraid of spiders, but not Anansi. He *loved* them—and they loved him too.

"What is it, Anansi?" asked Jack, noticing his friend's stormy expression. "I know we've all heard the poem a million times, but it's not *that* bad!"

"It's not the poem…it's *him*," hissed Anansi, nodding toward Mayor Fitch. "He *pretends* to be nice, but he can't be trusted! It's because of the trick he played on my uncle Rufaro and his troll friend Hurrilan when they were children that my family is cursed to look like trolls!"

"I *still* can't believe that Rufaro was friends with a troll when he was young," said Red. "Especially now that Hurrilan's the troll leader!"

"Back then Hurrilan was an outcast," explained Anansi. "He was living all alone in the woods, and he saved Rufaro's life, remember?" His voice was lost in the roar of the crowd as everyone became *very* excited.

The Sacred Shiny Story-Snipping Shears had just been brought out by the mayor's guards. There was a spell of protection on the Story Tree, and the only way *anything* could be cut from it was by using these magical shears. Mayor Fitch was holding them high above his head, preparing to make the first ceremonial snip, when a scream rose up through the crowd.

"*Trolls!*" someone yelled. "The trolls are coming!"

Immediately, Mayor Fitch's guards shot over to protect him, shoving the old lady who lived in a shoe into a muddy puddle. Jack and the others ran to help her as the rest of the crowd scattered.

In all the confusion, the mayor had dropped the Sacred Shiny Story-Snipping Shears, and nobody but Jack seemed to have noticed. As his hand reached out to pick up the shears, he was barged out of the way by a large, blue creature with webbed fingers and brightly glowing eyes.

"I'll take those!" said the creature, smiling a thin smile packed full of needle-sharp teeth. It waved its hand, and a torrent of water flooded over Jack and Betsy, sending them skidding backward over the ground.

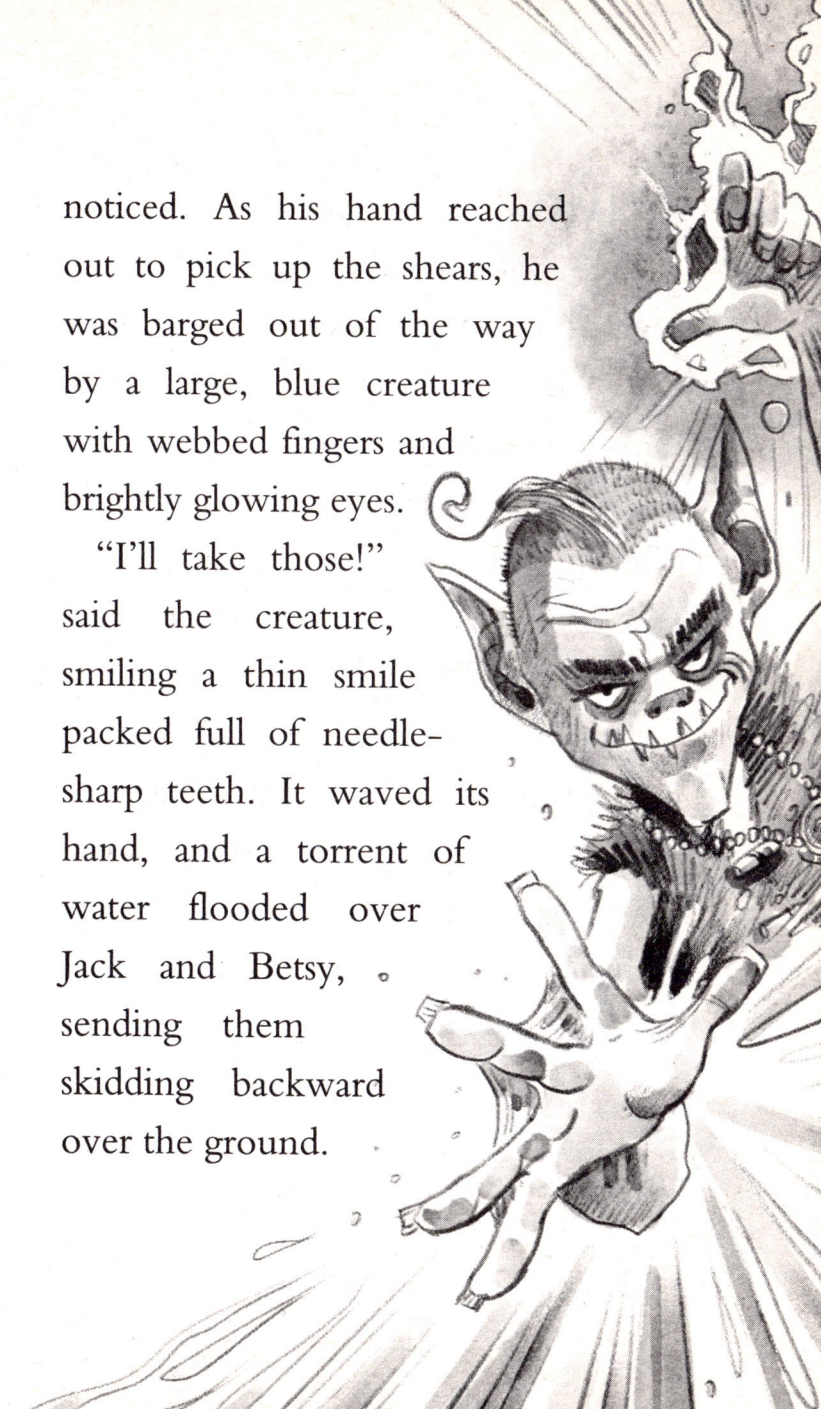

"**WHAAAAAT!?!**" gurgled Betsy.

"It's a water troll!" cried Jack as he struggled to get to his feet in the muddy water. "But how did it get past the Moonstone defenses?"

Moonstone was the only thing that kept trolls out of Tale Town. The enchanted rocks weakened the trolls' magic and made them feel dizzy and sick—but *something* had obviously gone wrong.

Using the shears, the water troll hacked down the freshest, newest sprout from the Story Tree, then sprinted off—taking the shears and the branch with him.

2
A Pale Imitation

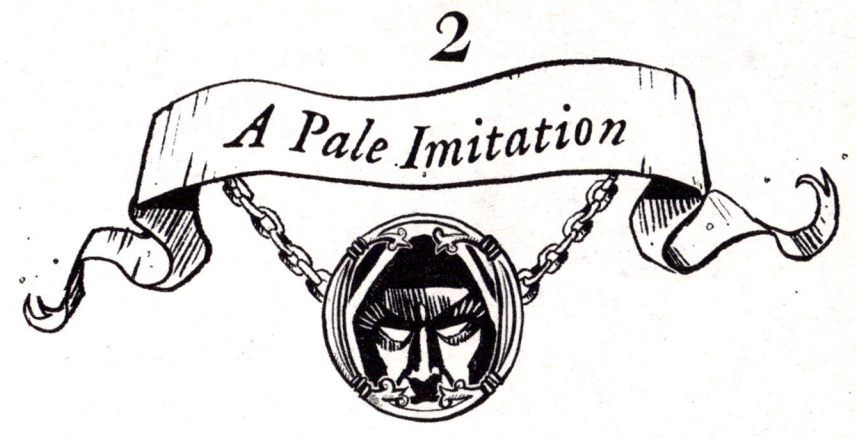

Far away in the mountains, at the very edge of the trolls' land, smoke from a small, flickering fire rose up through a hole in the center of a tent. Facing the fire was a large wooden throne covered in goatskins, upon which sprawled a tall, thin figure—a hooded cloak covering its face in darkness.

The entrance flap to the tent swung open, and a broad, stocky earth troll bustled in.

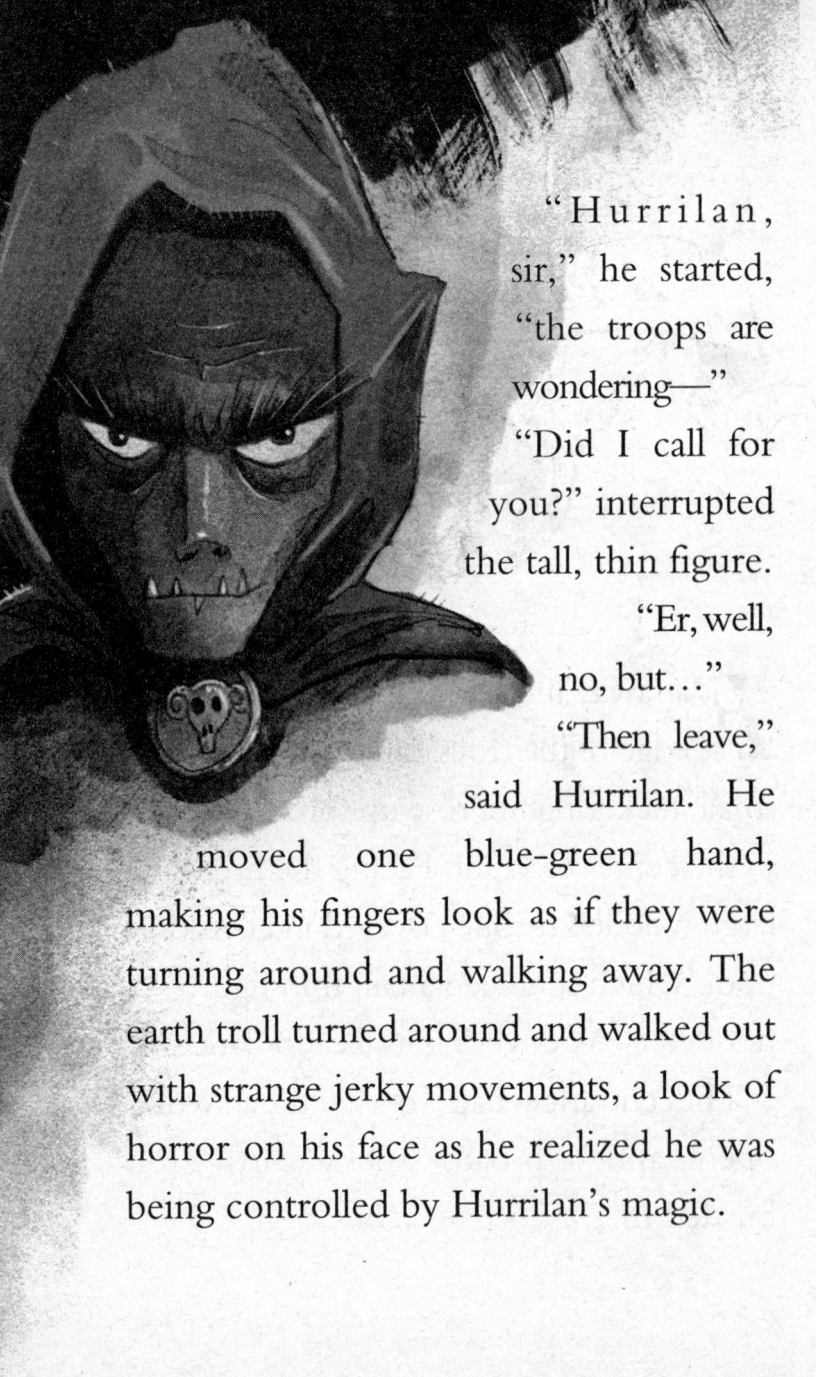

"Hurrilan, sir," he started, "the troops are wondering—"

"Did I call for you?" interrupted the tall, thin figure.

"Er, well, no, but…"

"Then leave," said Hurrilan. He moved one blue-green hand, making his fingers look as if they were turning around and walking away. The earth troll turned around and walked out with strange jerky movements, a look of horror on his face as he realized he was being controlled by Hurrilan's magic.

Moments later, a swirling light appeared in the middle of the tent and slowly formed into the shape of a man. He looked as though he was made of glass, almost completely see-through.

"You're late," snapped Hurrilan.

"Sorry," said the figure. "You know how it is. Things always take longer than…" He trailed off. "Still, I'm here now!" he added in a mumble.

"Will it work?" asked Hurrilan. "Will the branch from the Story Tree grow?"

"Definitely," replied the figure. "As long as your trolls can bring the branch to me before sunset, I can make it grow."

A smile crept across Hurrilan's face. "Excellent!" he exclaimed. "In that case, as soon as the branch takes root and you find a suitable host…*you* will get what *you* want."

The glass figure smiled greedily. "Thank you!" he said. "*Thank you* for this—"

Hurrilan waved a hand, and the transparent figure dissolved like a breaking wave. He leaned back slowly on his throne and smiled broadly. Soon, the trolls would have their *own* Story Tree. Soon, *their* stories would be heard.

───◆◆───

As soon as it was discovered that the Sacred Shiny Story-Snipping Shears and a branch from the Story Tree had been stolen, Mayor Fitch announced that everyone had to go home and stay in

their houses. The Moonstone defenses had been turned into mushrooms, which allowed the trolls to come in. That meant *someone* in Tale Town had allowed this to happen—someone with magic—and until the truth was discovered, *nobody* was allowed to do *anything*.

Rapunzel and her parents, the King and Queen, were away on an important royal engagement,* otherwise there was no way that the mayor would have gotten away with forcing everyone to stay at home—especially since Rapunzel's father often called Mayor

---

* The important royal engagement was actually a royal camping vacation—although, since Rapunzel's mother was a *very* light sleeper, she had ordered some servants to take apart their private bedchambers and rebuild them on the campsite, including all their furniture *and* bathrooms. So it wasn't *really* camping.

Fitch "that horribly slimy man" even when they were in the same room.

Red, Anansi, Jack, and Betsy were all being led back to their homes by one of Mayor Fitch's guards.

"This is crazy!" whispered Jack. "Nobody would let trolls in *on purpose!*"

"Perhaps..." replied Anansi. "But if you ask me, Sausage-Face Fitch is enjoying all this a little *too* much. You *know* how much he hates Rapunzel's parents. He wants to be completely in charge of Tale Town."

"But we *all* saw the trolls take the branch and the shears," said Red, looking sideways at the guard to make sure he wasn't listening. "Mayor Fitch certainly *looked* scared…"

"Well, *yeah*," started Anansi. "But that doesn't mean—"

"Silence!" barked the guard. "We'll have less talk and more walk! Do you think I've got nothing better to do?"

"Whaaaaaat!" said Betsy quietly, and Jack burst out laughing.

"*What?*" snapped the guard. "What's so funny?"

"Whaaaaaat…" added Betsy, her eyes glinting mischievously.

"Someone tell me what that bird just said," growled the guard, "or I'm havin' chicken nuggets for lunch tomorrow!"

"She just said that you *do* look *very* busy," said Jack, and the guard nodded self-importantly. "*Too busy to take a bath!*" Jack added in a whisper.

Red and Anansi snickered, and then Anansi said in a hushed voice, "Wait a minute… What happened to Hansel and Gretel?"

⋄ ◆ ⋄

Hansel and Gretel were walking through the woods outside Tale Town. As soon as the mayor's guards had started rounding people up, they had managed to slip silently away.

"What do you think is going on with Sausage-Face Fitch?" asked Hansel. "Why would he put the whole town on lockdown?"

"I don't know," replied Gretel. "I guess he thinks someone's helping the trolls. How about we—"

"—follow the troll's tracks? See if we can find out what's going on?" finished Hansel. "Good idea." He pointed down to a roughly snapped branch and a large footprint on the forest floor.

"This is almost *too* easy!" said Gretel, then paused. "Do you think we should tell Dad what we're doing?"

"I thought he was off on vacation with our new stepmom, Valerie?"

"Oh yeah! I forgot. I thought she was called Susan though?"

"No, Susan was last year," corrected Hansel. "Then there was Andrea then Atsuko and *now* Valerie. She's *OK*, I guess… Not

as bossy as Susan—and nowhere *near* as mean as Atsuko."

"She was the *worst!*" agreed Gretel. "Always sending us off on those picnics in Bear Maul Woods and those swimming trips in Piranha Lagoon! Wasn't it weird that she always forgot to bring her *own* swimming things?"

They walked on in silence for a while, wondering who it was that decided that *all* stepmothers in the Fairy Tale Kingdom had to be awful. It was a *really* annoying law.

3
A Sheep in Wolf's Clothing

The twins had been following the trolls' trail for almost half a day. They had stopped by a babbling brook to have something to eat, but the brook just kept *on* babbling. At first they'd listened politely—but it just wouldn't stop talking—so they'd crept silently away.

They were walking on through the woods when Gretel stopped abruptly and sniffed the air.

SNIFFFFFF!

"*Wolves!*" she hissed. "I can smell them." She stopped and sniffed again, then frowned, looking confused.

"I can smell something else too..." Hansel added. "Is that—"

"—*fabric softener?*" said Gretel. They looked at each other, then crept through the bushes toward the scent.

In the middle of a small clearing sat a wolf. He was young, little more than a cub, and he didn't look very scary— partly because his face looked so open and gentle, and his fur seemed so soft that it might have been blow-dried. But mainly because he was wearing a stylish little cap and had a handkerchief tied around his neck.

"You can come out if you want," said the wolf. "I can hear you rustling around."

"Oh…er—"

"—right…will do," said Hansel and Gretel as they scrambled out of the bushes.

"Are you from Tale Town?" asked the wolf.

Hansel and Gretel looked at each other, having one of their silent, eyebrow-wiggling conversations as they tried to figure out whether they could trust this wolf cub. Like trolls, wolves were *bad news* in Tale Town, but this young cub seemed different.

"Yes," they said eventually. "We are."

"Oh, I would *love* to visit Tale Town!"

said the wolf wistfully. "Just imagine… The excitement! The cafés! The parties! But my dad won't allow it. He's always like, '*Wolves are wolves, son! We're not like them. We eat, we scheme, we steal, we go to the toilet OUTSIDE in the woods, and we don't, for ANY reason, use toilet paper.*'" The young wolf wrinkled his nose. "Seriously! He expects me to use *leaves* or something. It's totally gross!"

"You're not like any of the other wolves I've ever met," said Hansel. "You seem so much more…"

"Soft? Lame? Feeble? Un-terrifying? *Pathetic?*" asked the wolf. "*Yes*, I've heard it all before…"

"I was going to say *nice*, actually," said Hansel. "Anyway, I'm Hansel, and this is Gretel."

"I'm Wolfson, born of Greymist, grandson of Throat-Rip the Destroyer," replied the wolf. "But I prefer *Wolfie*. I've never liked having Throat-Rip in my name. So *aggressive*!"

"I suppose so," said Gretel with a smile.

"So, what are you doing out here?" asked Wolfie. "You're a long way from home."

Hansel and Gretel told Wolfie all about what had happened

back in Tale Town—how the trolls had stolen a branch from the Story Tree along with the sacred shears and how the mayor had put the whole town on lockdown until he got to the bottom of it all. They explained that they were going to try to get back the shears *and* the branch.

Wolfie's eyes flashed with excitement. "Oh, I would *love* to do something like that!" he said. "Doing something *good*, for once! I'm always saying to Dad, 'We should try to make friends in Tale Town, you know? Stop swallowing up grandmothers whole. People just don't like that sort of thing, it makes them feel sad. Why would you *want* to make people sad?'"

"I always thought it was—"

"—instinct or something?" said Hansel and Gretel.

"Well, *maybe*," said Wolfie. "But *no more*! I'm going to show Tale Town that not all wolves are bloodthirsty granny gobblers and pig-tricking cheaters and liars! I'm going to come with you! I'm going to prove that wolves…can be *good*!" He paused, slightly out of breath after his speech. "Er, that's as long as you guys don't mind if I tag along?"

The twins laughed. "The more, the merrier!" they said in unison.

"Do you need to get anything before we go?" asked Gretel.

"Actually, it's probably best if I don't go back home

first," replied Wolfie. "Dad might ask questions and—"

"*Wolfson!*" roared a deep, growling voice through the trees.

Wolfie's eyes shot wide open. "It's Dad!" he whispered frantically. "*Hide!*"

"Who you talkin' to?" demanded the voice, getting closer now. "I can smell *'umans*!"

Wolfie's eyes twitched this way and that as he tried to figure out what to do. Then he had an idea. "Run!" he whispered. "*As fast as you can!*"

"It's...er, humans all right, Dad!" he shouted back to his father. "I was tracking them forever and now you scared them off!"

"Well, I declare! I'm sorry," bellowed

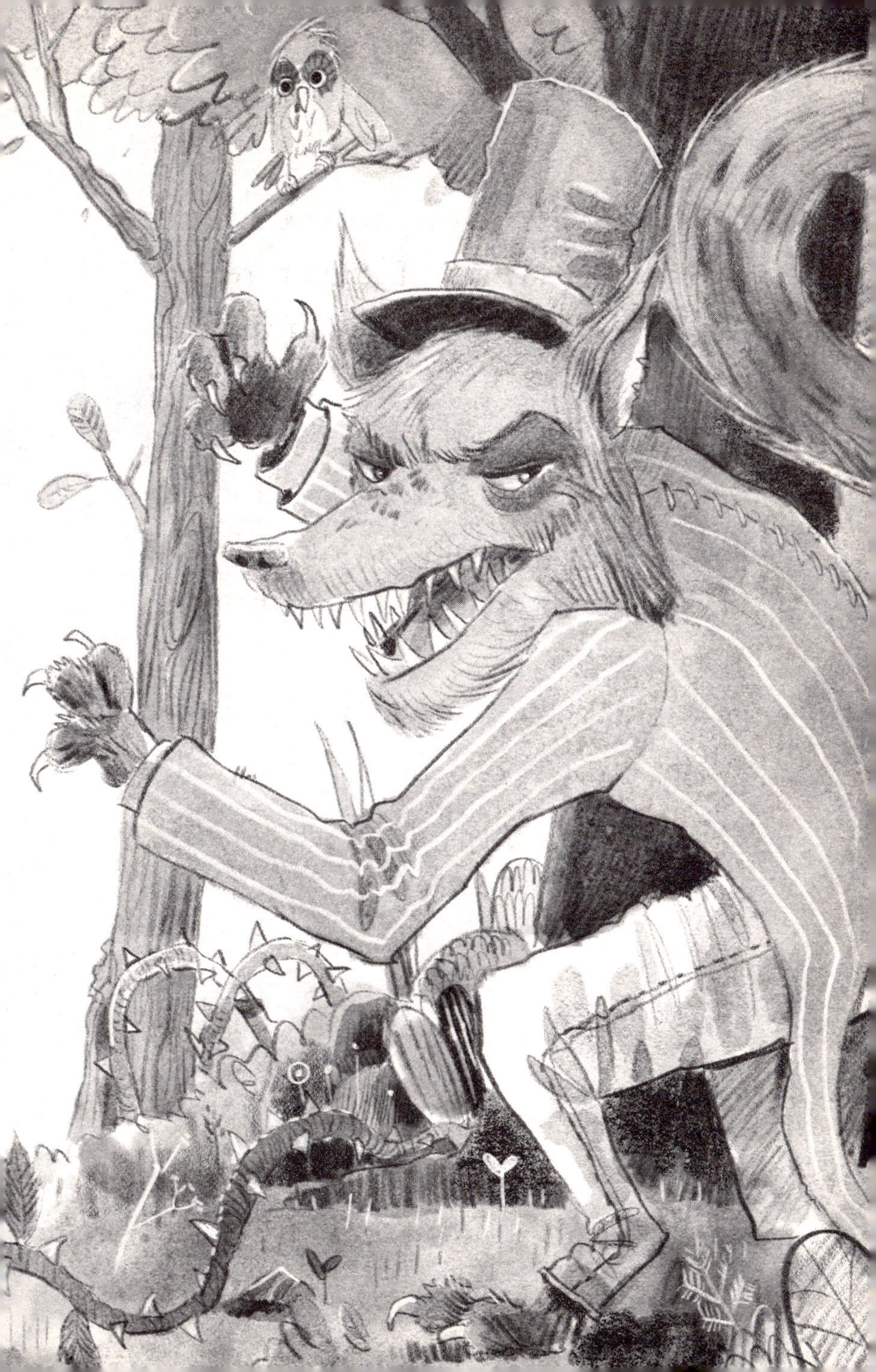

the huge, grizzled gray wolf as he burst into the clearing. "I didn't realize. Still, we can catch 'em and tear them apart *together*."

"Um, thanks, Dad," said Wolfie. "But this is something I really want to do *myself*. I'll, er…totally gut them and…" He paused uncertainly. "Wear their toes as a necklace?"

"Good boy, Wolfson!" chuckled Wolfie's dad, or as most people called him, the Big Bad Wolf. "I *always* knew you had it in yer!"

4
The Green Man's Lair

Hansel and Gretel always thought they were the *best* at following trails, tracks, bread crumbs, stones, or the delicious scent of gingerbread—but that was before they met Wolfie. He might not have enjoyed some of the more grisly things about being a wolf, but it *did* give him an amazing sense of smell and hearing. It wasn't long before they found themselves outside a huge wooden wall that grew right out of the ground.

"What is—"

"—this place?" wondered Hansel and Gretel. Brambles were woven in and around the living wall. Thorns the size of hands spiked dangerously outward.

"I've been here before," said Wolfie thoughtfully. "But it didn't look like this! The wall was much lower, and there were lots of plants and flowers growing everywhere. The Green Man lived here, a kind of nature wizard. He loved *everything* about nature—even wolves! But now it feels so *unfriendly*."

"And, this is where—"

"—the trail ends?" asked Hansel and Gretel.

"Afraid so," said Wolfie, shivering a little. "So I guess we'd better go back and tell someone else? You know, like someone big, with weapons and an army and stuff?"

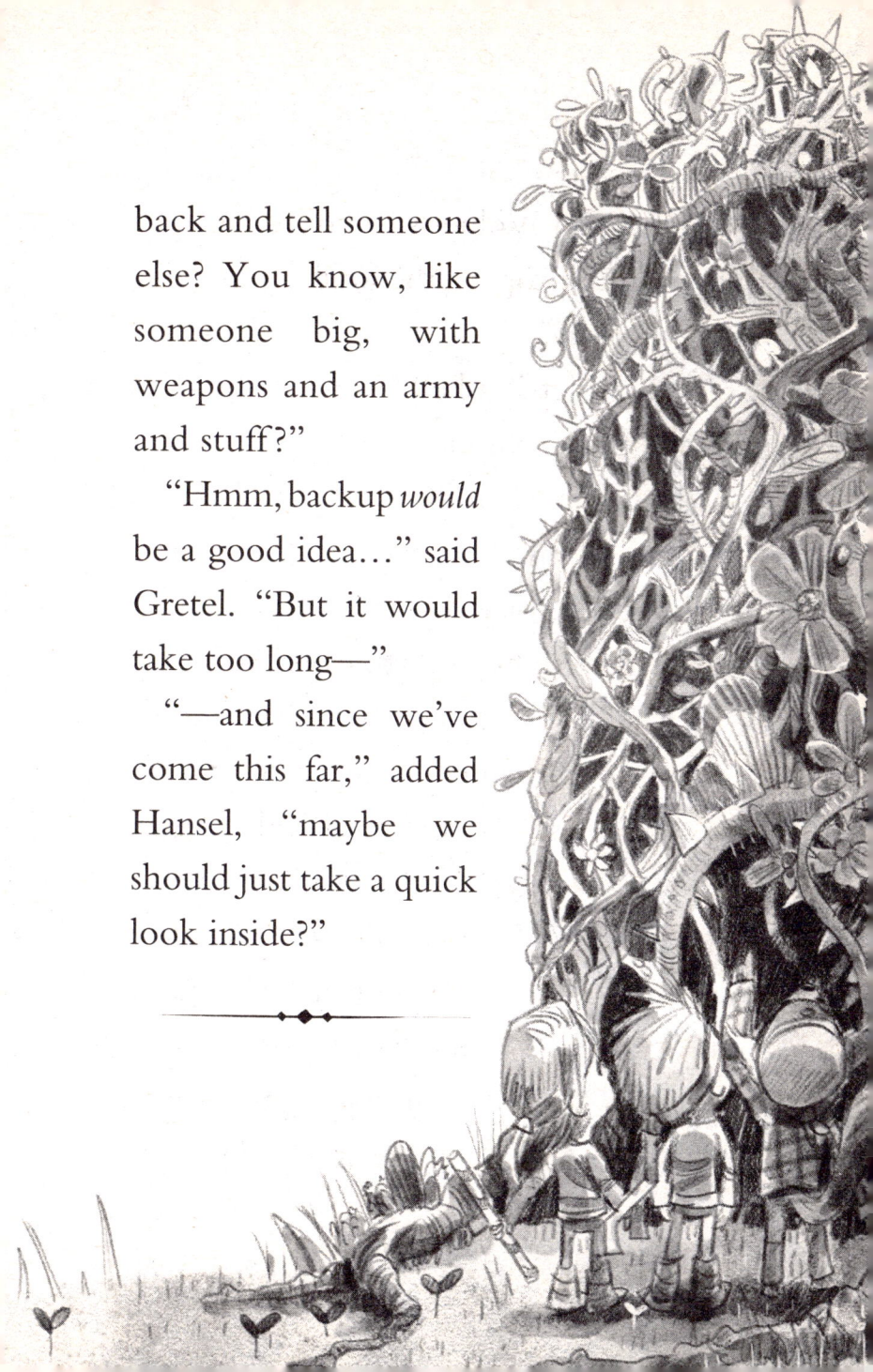

"Hmm, backup *would* be a good idea…" said Gretel. "But it would take too long—"

"—and since we've come this far," added Hansel, "maybe we should just take a quick look inside?"

"Wow!" said Wolfie as he poked his head up over the top of the wall. "Just, you know...*wow*!"

"What is it?" asked Hansel, who was climbing up behind him.

"It's *troll central* in there!" replied Wolfie. "I don't think I've ever seen so many trolls, outside of a *Where's Trollo?* book!"

There were huge earth trolls with dull green skin and thick, muscular bodies and blue water trolls with scales and webbed fingers and toes. There were even a few wind trolls, tall and thin, with long hair that billowed out even when the air was perfectly still.

"What are they all doing here together?" asked Hansel. "I thought the different troll clans didn't really get along."

"No idea!" replied Gretel. "But forget *that*. How are we going to find the branch from the Story Tree?"

"Forget *that*!" said Wolfie. "How are we even going to get *in*?"

On the other side of the wall was a large courtyard filled with ferocious statues of wild animals. Trolls milled around, carrying crates of supplies and weapons or just sitting around playing cards. In the middle of the courtyard rose a huge, living palace. It was made in the same way as the wall they were perched on—trees and plants had knitted together and grown into towers, rooms, roofs, and windows. The whole thing was covered with a tangled mass of dark, thorny brambles.

"We have to split up," said Gretel. "We'll get spotted for *sure* if we try to get in together, but if we go one by one, we *should* be OK."

Wolfie shuddered at the use of the word *should*. "How about I wait here?" he suggested. "And keep lookout?"

"We'll cover more ground if we all go in," said Gretel firmly.

"Mmm, right," muttered Wolfie. "Is there a secret signal to use if we get into trouble?"

"How about we bleat like a goat?" suggested Hansel.

"A *goat*?" asked Wolfie. "Are you serious? Trolls *eat* goats. They'll come running!"

"Good point," said Hansel. "How about a raccoon?"

"What do *they* even sound like?" asked Gretel.

"An owl?" suggested Wolfie.

"It's the middle of the day!" protested Hansel and Gretel.

"All right," said Wolfie sarcastically. "How about we just yell, '*Help! I'm in trouble!*'?"

"Works for me," replied Hansel. "I guess if things get *that* bad, then it won't really matter anyway!"

Hansel and Gretel looked bright-eyed and excited. Wolfie looked like he was going to be sick.

———◆◆———

Hansel climbed silently down the thorn-covered wall. He moved like water, flowing from hiding place to hiding place. It was as though he knew *exactly* where each troll was, without even having to look. Within seconds, he had dashed over to the wooden palace. He paused to give a quick thumbs-up to Gretel and Wolfie, before inching a door open and slipping inside.

"Whoa! How did he *do* that?" asked Wolfie. "That was *amazing!*"

Gretel shrugged. "When you spend enough time on your own, you get good at looking after yourself! But you'd know all about that sort of thing, being a wolf, right?" She grinned at Wolfie as she scrambled down the wall, darting across the courtyard and taking cover behind a barrel. When there were no trolls looking, she shot across to a pile of crates near a large locked door and managed to climb up to an open window without making a sound. She twisted in through the small opening and disappeared from sight.

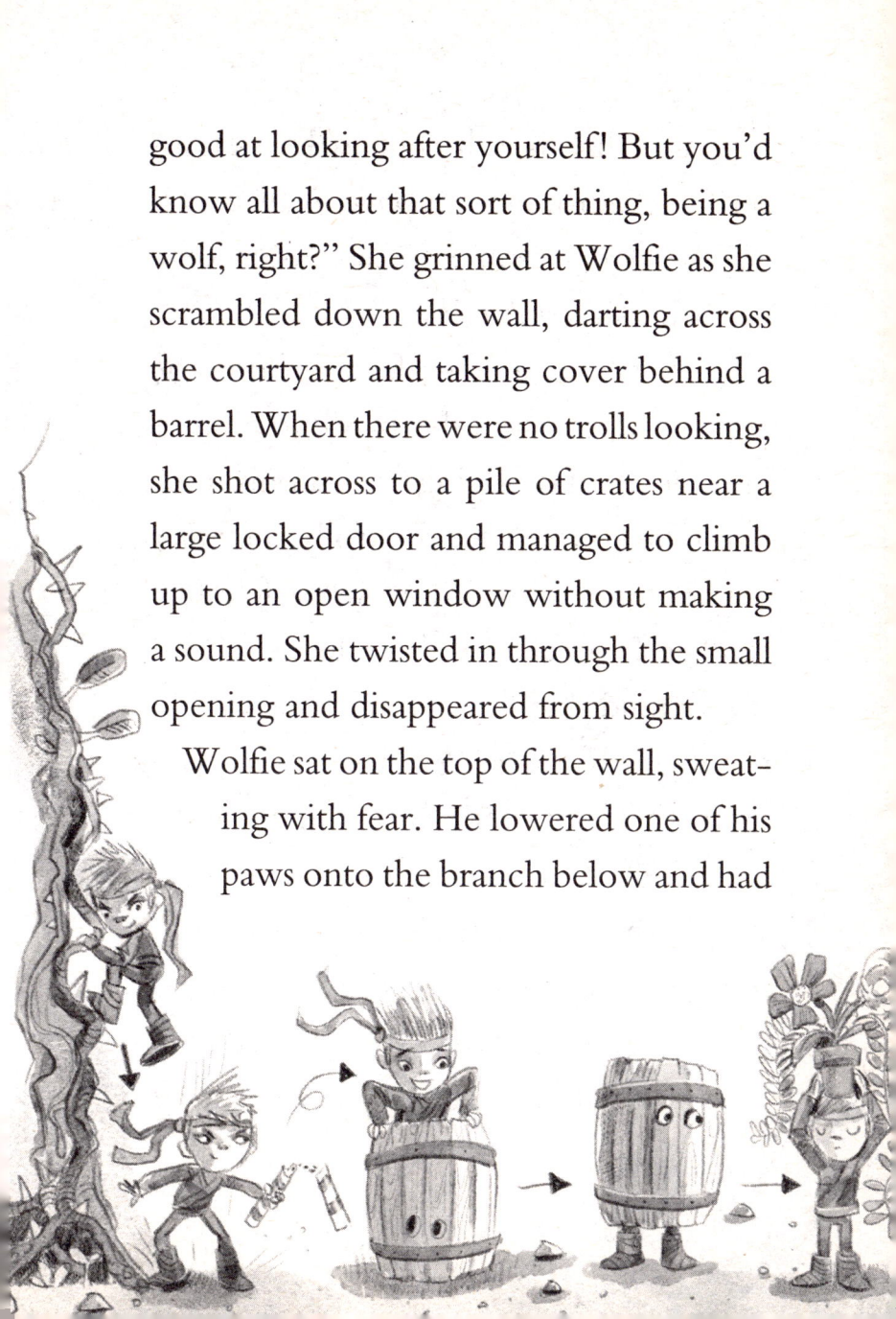

Wolfie sat on the top of the wall, sweating with fear. He lowered one of his paws onto the branch below and had to clamp his mouth shut as he stepped on a big thorn. He was *probably* bleeding! Maybe he'd get rabies or tetanus or some other horrible infection…

After taking a few deep breaths, he continued on clumsily, hardly daring to look down and hoping with all his heart that if he couldn't see the trolls, then *they* couldn't see him. After what felt like forever, he finally had both feet safely on the ground. He hid behind a big pile of ropes and wondered what he was going to do next. Just then a bell rang out and a voice bellowed, *"Dinner's ready!"*

All the trolls hurried off into a small, leafy cafeteria building, chattering about what they hoped was going to be for dinner and, if there was going to be dessert, whether it would be goat ice cream—which they all seemed to agree was their favorite.

Wolfie watched one last hungry-looking troll lope into the cafeteria. Aside from the scary animal statues, the whole place was completely deserted. He smiled slightly as he crept out of his hiding place and scampered across the courtyard.

Hansel made his way down a long, dark tunnel. He strained his ears for the sound of any approaching trolls, but could hear nothing. The corridor was uneven, and plants and ferns grew everywhere, blocking his way. He tiptoed along, not knowing exactly what he was looking for, but hoping that he'd know it when he saw it. What he *wasn't* expecting to find was Gretel. They both silently crept around a corner and came face-to-face with each other, eyes wide with surprise.

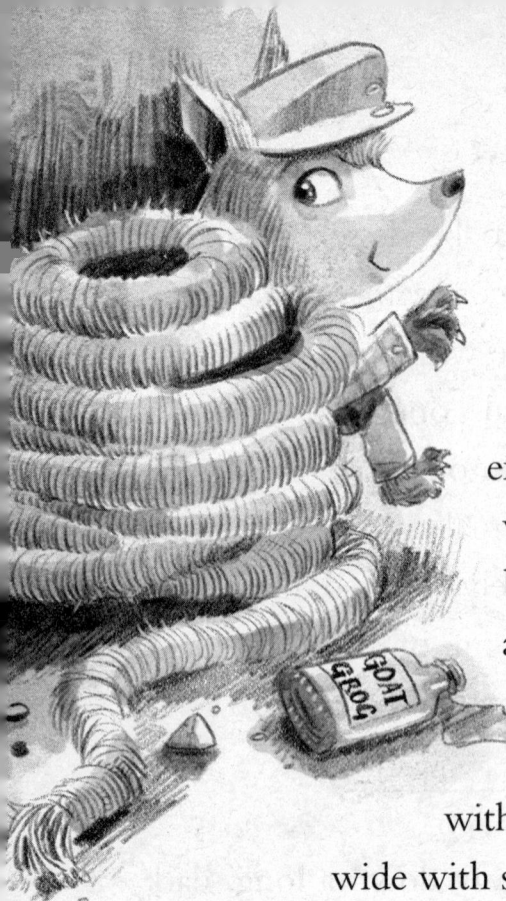

Hansel wiggled one eyebrow to mean: *Have you seen any trolls?*

Gretel shifted her eyes to the left to reply: *No, I haven't seen a single troll since I came in.*

Hansel wrinkled his nose to say: *Me*

either. Maybe it's only the outside that's guarded?

Gretel grinned and shrugged to say: *Then why aren't we talking out loud?*

"No idea!" whispered Hansel. "Come on. Let's see what we can see!"

Together they explored the living palace, looking in every room. Just as they were approaching the end of a corridor, there was a blue-gray blur as something disappeared around the corner.

"What was *that*?" asked Hansel.

"I have no idea—" began Gretel.

"*Help!*" interrupted a nearby voice. "Please, you *must* help me!"

Gretel shot a worried look at her brother.

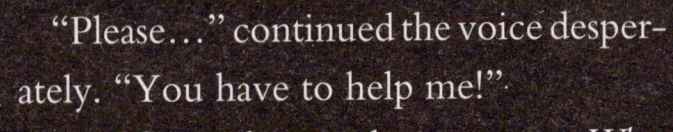

"Please..." continued the voice desperately. "You have to help me!"

Gretel raised an eyebrow to say: *What should we do?*

Hansel narrowed his eyes, meaning: *We'd better investigate!*

―――◆―――

The twins peered into a room

that was empty, except for a large golden mirror. It had curling decorations all around the frame and a glassy surface that shifted and swirled with different colors. In the mirror was the reflection of a man—even though the room was empty.

"Whoa!" breathed Hansel. "A magic looking glass!"

The figure in the mirror peered out with scared eyes. "Oh, please say that you'll help," it begged. "Please!"

"Why?" asked Gretel from the doorway. "What's happened?"

"It's my master, the Green Man!" gasped the mirror. "The trolls have placed him under a spell and are using his powers to keep a branch alive from a tree that can grow stories!"

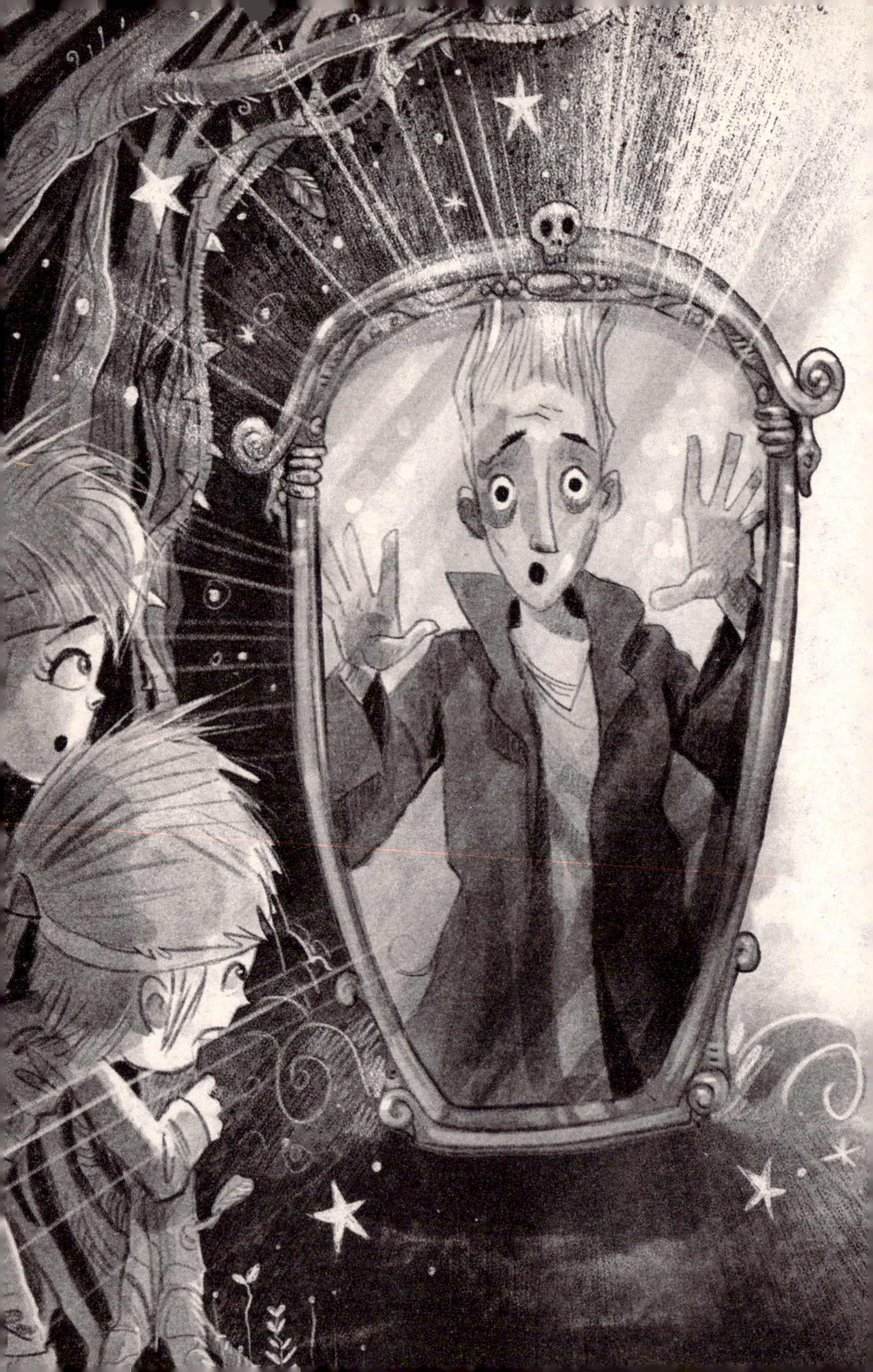

"We know that the trolls took a branch from the Story Tree," exclaimed Hansel.

"We saw it happen!" added Gretel.

"I know where the branch is being kept!" said the mirror. "*You* have to help me get the branch away from here, so I can break the trolls' spell and free my master. Will you help?"

"If we *do* help—" began Gretel.

"—can we take the branch back to Tale Town?" finished Hansel.

"Of course!" said the mirror. "I just want my master back. So you'll help me?"

Hansel and Gretel looked at each other. "Yes," they said. "We will."

"Marvelous!" exclaimed the mirror. "Well, come in, *come in!*"

5
Body Snatcher

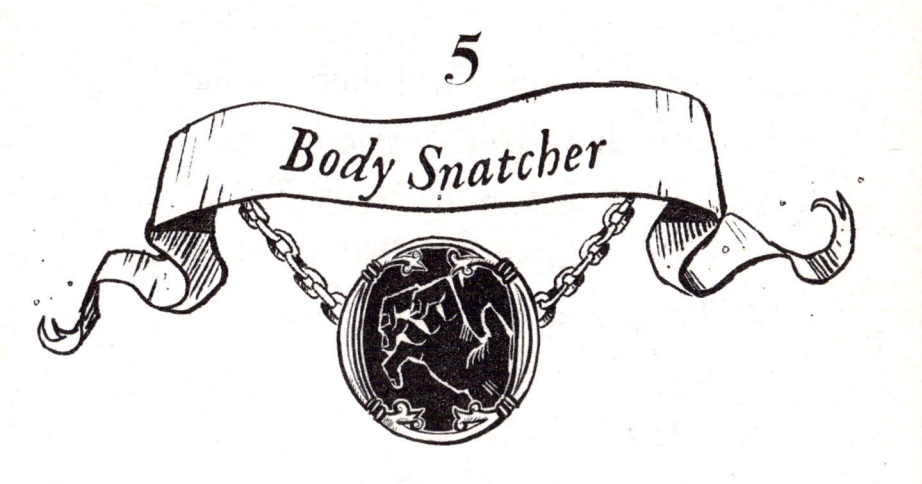

Hansel and Gretel stood in the doorway, looking at the magic mirror. The figure behind the glass smiled warmly at them. "Sorry...could you both just come a little closer please?" it asked. "My eyesight's not what it used to be."

"OK," said Gretel as they walked into the room. "So...where's the branch?"

"Gosh! Aren't you *clever*?" exclaimed

the mirror. "I must say, I simply couldn't do this without you! *Fnnnnrrp!*"

"Sorry, what was that?" asked Hansel.

"What was *what*?" replied the mirror.

"That sort of *snort*," said Gretel.

"Like you were trying not to laugh?" added Hansel.

"Oh, *that*?" replied the mirror. "No, no, no…it's just…I get hay fever at this time of year."

"*Right…*" said Hansel, glancing over at Gretel suspiciously.

Suddenly, the door swung shut behind them with a loud bang, and the mirror laughed a long and horrible laugh. "*Ha!*" exclaimed the mirror. "*Now* you are at my mercy!" The reflection paused and patted down all its pockets. "Now, where did I put my mercy? I'm *sure* I put it somewhere? Oh, yes! Now I remember! I don't have any. I am mercy-less! *Merciless!*" It laughed again.

"Wow, that was the lamest joke *ever*!" whispered Hansel.

"Yeah!" agreed Gretel. "Come on. *Let's get out of here!*"

They turned to run out of the room, but their legs stiffened and slowed down, until they couldn't move at all.

Hansel gave Gretel a look that said: *This isn't good!*

Gretel thought a message back to her brother: *Shall we use the secret signal?*

Hansel nodded in agreement, and then they both yelled as loud as they could: "Help! We're in trouble!"

◆

Wolfie frowned as he padded down *another* empty corridor. It was as though the wooden palace was completely deserted. He'd seen no sign of the Green Man or any trolls, but *that* wasn't a bad thing. He wasn't entirely sure what his plan would be if he was spotted by a troll, but he thought it would probably involve quite a lot of running away and screaming "*AAAaaaaarrrrghhhh.*"

A distant sound made Wolfie's hair

stand up on end. He could hear the signal for help echoing down the corridors.

"*Help! We're in trouble!*"

With barely a thought for his safety—except for the obvious things, like how he *really* didn't want to get trapped or hurt or kidnapped or eaten or squashed or bruised or anything horrible like that—Wolfie turned and ran to help his friends.

Neither Hansel nor Gretel could move their legs at all. They stood there, frozen, as the door swung open and a few blue-gray imps scampered into the room and dragged the mirror around on a small wheeled cart so it was facing them again.

"Nice of you to *stick around*," said the magic mirror.

"What do you want?" asked Hansel coldly.

"Well...*you*, I suppose," replied the mirror. "You see, I've always been rather held back by the whole 'magic looking glass' thing. I mean, I can leave for a short while…"

Hansel and Gretel both gasped as the reflection stepped out of the mirror, right in front of them.

"But it's not *enough!*" complained the reflection, swiping its hand soundlessly through Hansel's chest, making him flinch although he felt nothing.

"I can't *actually* touch anything!" explained the reflection. "I'm not *really* real! But with one of your bodies, and my troll friend's help? Well, then I can be real—and it will be *you* rotting away in this mirror instead!"

───◆───

Wolfie's breath came in gasps as he ran

as fast as he could down the hallway, knocking over plant pots and breaking saplings that grew up from the floor. From behind a half-open door ahead he could hear a voice he didn't recognize saying, "All I have to do is summon the troll warlock, and then I will be free of this mirror—*forever*! I'll be able to dance outside in the rain and *feel* the wind on my face! I'll be able to actually *smell* flowers as I brush my hand against them *and* kick down small children's sandcastles—it's going to be *amazing*!"

Wolfie held his breath as he pressed himself flat against the wall and peered through the doorway. Hansel and Gretel looked very uncomfortable—their legs were frozen in a running position.

"You'll never take my body!" yelled Hansel.

"Or mine!" spat Gretel.

"Oh, but I will!" said the mirror. "I can do whatever I like! Watch this: I shall swap your personalities! As simply as...this!" The reflection laughed as it pointed at each twin and then crossed its hands over. A glow trailed from each hand, swirling around Hansel and Gretel's heads, and for a moment, both of their faces went limp.

The reflection clicked its fingers. "There! You have had your personalities switched! Your minds are in the wrong bodies! I can only imagine the *horror*! The *fear* you must feel! *Now* do you see? *Now* do you feel the *awful* depths of my power?"

6
Role Reversal

Wolfie looked around. He had to do *something* to help. But what? He didn't have any tools or weapons. It was *hopeless*! Then he spotted a wooden bucket of muddy water.

I wonder... he thought as he grabbed the bucket.

Inside the room, the reflection gazed expectantly at the twins and then frowned.

"Whoa!" said Gretel from Hansel's

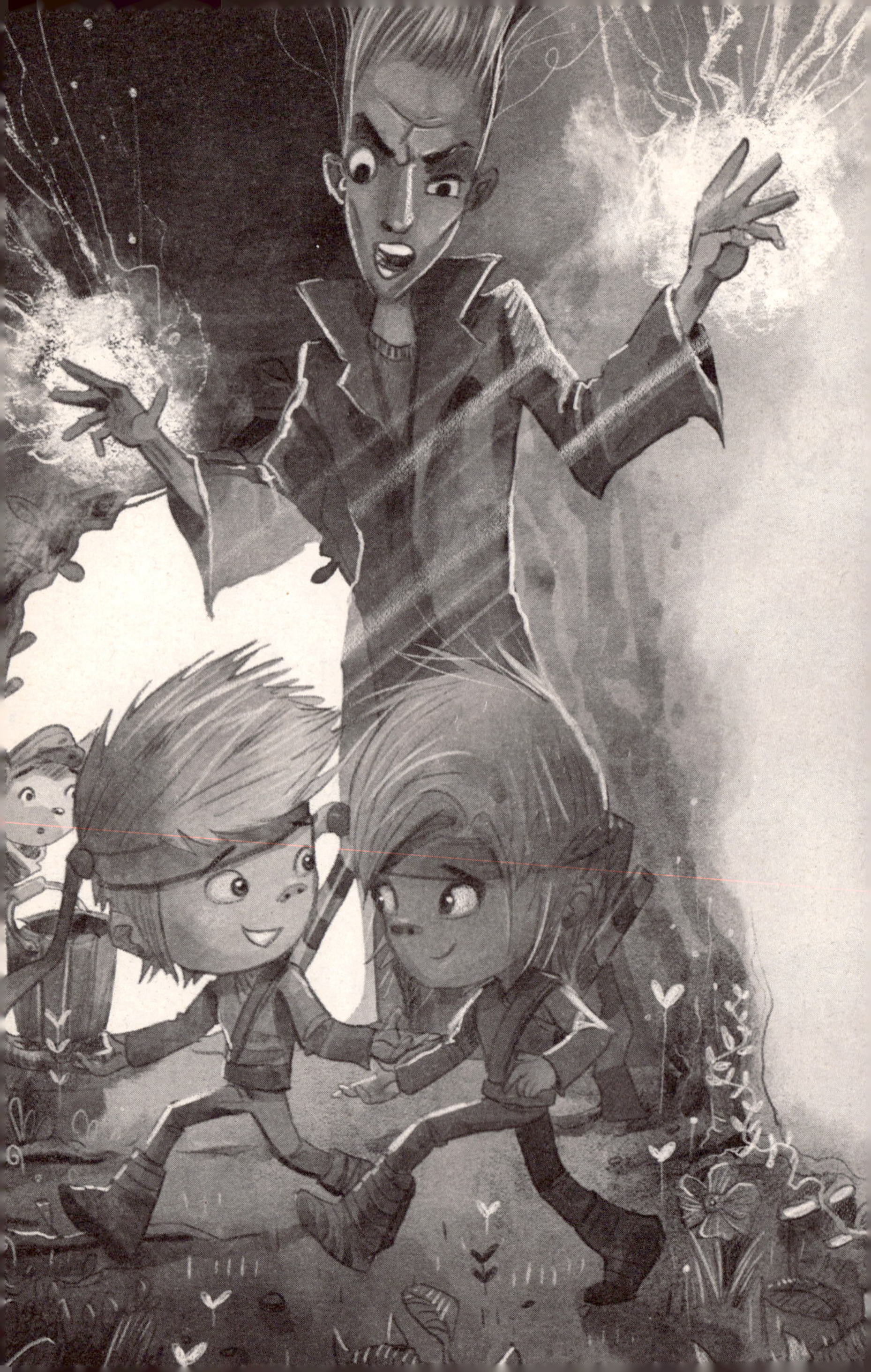

body. "This is kind of weird. I never realized that you didn't like broccoli."

"No, not really..." admitted Hansel from Gretel's body. "It looks a little too much like a tiny tree, you know what I mean? Anyway, I like how you have your hair a little longer. It feels nice!"

"*No, no, no, NO!*" shrieked the mirror. "This isn't right! You're meant to be paralyzed with fear, begging for mercy!"

"Well, you already made that lame joke about not having any—" said Gretel.

"—so what's the point?" finished Hansel. "Besides, *you* don't scare us! We've dealt with worse creatures than you!"

"*Really?*" asked the reflection. "Worse than me?"

"Yeah!" said Gretel. "Together we can do anything!"

The reflection grinned. "Well then, let's see how you like it when you can't do *anything* together!" The reflection pointed at the twins again, a glowing light snaking from its hands toward them. The light grew brighter until, with a brief, blinding flash, it fell away.

Hansel and Gretel were back in their own bodies and free to move again. But instead of looking happy, they looked furious.

"This is all *your* fault!" shouted Gretel at Hansel.

"No way!" hissed Hansel. "It's *your* fault! I don't know why I've put up with you for so long!"

The reflection smiled wickedly.

"I'm going to do something I should have done a long time ago!" muttered Gretel, taking a step toward Hansel waving her candy-cane staff in the air.

"Suits me!" said Hansel. "It's *about time* somebody taught you some manners!" He pulled his candy-cane nunchucks off his back and swirled them through the air.

The reflection gurgled with delight. "So *now* do you feel my pow*arghhhhhh!*"

There was a loud muddy splash as a huge bucket of filthy water was flung over the mirror, completely covering the glass. Wolfie hurled the bucket at the glass as hard as he could, but it just bounced off.

"You fool!" yelled the reflection. "You can't break a magic mirror! I am *indestructible!*" It tried to look toward Wolfie, but was just as filth-covered as the mirror and fumbled blindly about. "Where are you?" it demanded, trying to wipe the mud from its face. "I will find you. Don't you worry about that! And when I do, I'll swap your eyeballs for eggs! *Rotten ones!*"

"Come on, you two!" yelled Wolfie to the twins. "We've got to get out of here!"

"Thank goodness somebody sensible's turned up!" said Gretel.

"*You'll regret this…*" cried the mirror.

"Hey, Wolfie?" said Hansel as though he hadn't heard anything the mirror had said. "Can you tell my sister that if she's trying to annoy me, she's doing a good job?"

"I'll find out if you like mayonnaise or not! And if you don't, I'll bury you up to your neck in it…" continued the mirror.

"Oh, really!" said Gretel, ignoring the mirror's threats. "Well, Wolfie, can you please inform my brother, that I couldn't give a—"

She stopped speaking as Wolfie grabbed them both by the hand and dragged them out of the room.

"Seriously! Once that mirror gets cleaned up, it is not going to be happy!" yelled Wolfie. "We've got to go—now!"

"Come on! Hurry up!" cried the reflection as a handful of imps struggled to wipe the dirt off the mirror's surface. "He'll be here any minute, and I still look filthy."

"Who will be here?" called a voice from a dark corner of the room.

"Gah!" shrieked the reflection, leaping high into the air and then trying to make it look as though it had just been doing some exercises. Out of the shadows stepped a magical projection of the troll Hurrilan, flickering in the dim light.

"Hurrilan! How *lovely* it is to see you!" the reflection exclaimed, shooing its imp underlings away. "What an honor!"

"Be quiet," said Hurrilan, and the reflection fell silent. "The branch. Is it growing? You've managed to use your master's magic?" The reflection nodded, and Hurrilan looked pleased. "That's good news," he said. "When the Green Man refused to help me, I thought that was the end…but with *your* help, it seems we will have our own Story Tree—at last! *Everything* is going according to plan!"

"Mmm..." said the reflection.

"Sorry, what was that?"

"Yes, it's *almost* all going perfectly!"

"*Almost?* Is the branch safe: yes or no?" asked Hurrilan.

"Yes-*ish*?" said the reflection in a small voice.

Hurrilan glared at him. "Let's try this one more time... You have the branch. It is growing, and everything is OK?"

"Yes, *but...*" began the reflection. Then it noticed Hurrilan's expression and finished off with, "But *actually*, now that I think about it...everything's *great!*"

"Glad to hear it," said the troll warlock,

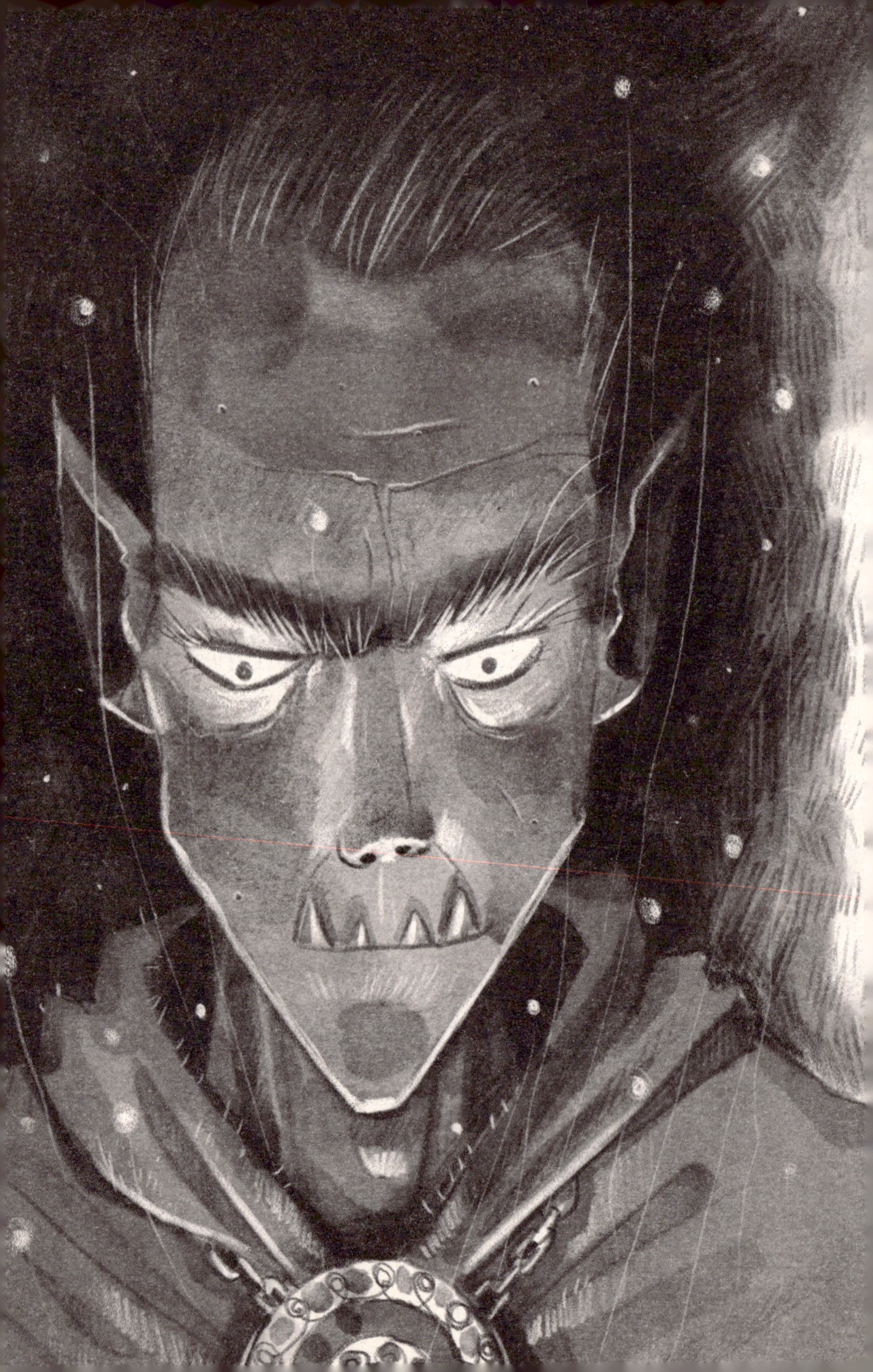

nodding. "*Please* make sure that you take *extremely* good care of that branch. If *anything* were to happen to it, I would be *most* distressed."

The mirror bobbed nervously. "Yes—yes, of course!" it said.

Hurrilan narrowed his eyes. "I sometimes do things I regret when I'm upset," he said. "*Awful* things… Do we understand each other?"

The reflection nodded and gulped nervously as the image of Hurrilan vanished.

"Hey, Wolfie?" said Hansel. "Can you ask my sister to walk downwind of me? It's *really* starting to smell around here."

"Oh, Wolfie?" said Gretel. "Guess what? I've invented a brand-new word for *stupid,* and you spell it like this: H-A-N-S-E-L."

Hansel pretended to laugh. "Oh, that's *soooooo* funny, so *completely* hilarious! Wolfie? Can you *please* tell my—"

"*No!*" shouted Wolfie. Hansel and Gretel fell silent. Wolfie *tried* to glare at them like his dad, the Big Bad Wolf, glared at people, but the effect wasn't *quite* the same. His quivering little snout made him look confused, worried, and upset. Gretel patted him on the shoulder.

"Sorry, Wolfie," she said. "I didn't mean to upset you."

"You two have *got* to figure this out!"

said Wolfie. "We're on a mission, *remember*?"

"Absolutely!" exclaimed Hansel. "And we're *totally* going to succeed! Just as soon as we get rid of my deadweight of a sister!"

"Oh, it's like *that*, is it?" yelled Gretel. "Well, *fine*! Me and Wolfie were just leaving! Weren't we, Wolfie?"

"I don't *think* so!" snorted Hansel. "Wolfie is coming with *me*! Right, Wolfie?"

Wolfie groaned. It was *exactly* the same with his dad and the people of

Tale Town—he was *always* caught in the middle. Well, *no more*! Wolfie was going to put his foot down.

"No!" he said firmly. "We are not splitting up! And stop arguing about who gets to keep me. I'm not your *pet*!" He stood there with his paws on his hips, his furry tail wagging behind him and his whiskers trembling. "We're *all* going to have to find a way to get through this *together*! I mean, you know…so long as that's OK with you guys?"

7
Be Your Own Wolf

The plan was to track the imps' movements so they could figure out where the branch was. *Then* the plan was to take back the branch and sneak out without being seen. It was Wolfie's plan, and everyone agreed it was a good one.

But it seemed that carrying out the plan wasn't going to be that easy. Gretel was silently tracking one of the imps when

Hansel fired a shot from his slingshot and made her trip. The only reason that the imp didn't see her was because she happened to fall right into a pile of compost. Later, while Hansel had been climbing a rope to get to one of the higher levels of the palace, Gretel had fired a burning arrow that set fire to the rope, and Hansel had to slide back down as quickly as he could.

"What?" Gretel had protested when Wolfie glared at her. "It was an accident!"

Next, Wolfie had to stop Hansel from trying to glue Gretel's hands to a doorknob and Gretel from chaining Hansel to a pillar.

"This is no good!" exploded Wolfie. "We'll never find the branch like this! You two are going to get us all captured!"

Then a thought occurred to him. It was quite a sneaky thought, and it almost surprised him. He didn't normally "do" sneaky, but maybe there was more wolf in him than he realized.

"Hey, guys…" said Wolfie. "Which one of you would be better at finding your way home? You know, if you were trapped in a forest and only had a handful of bread crumbs or something?"

"That would be me," began Hansel. "Although I'd have to say that bread crumbs are *not* an effective way of marking a route. What you *really* need are white pebbles, then—"

"What on earth are you talking about?" interrupted Gretel. "Firstly, *I* am clearly the superior trail finder. Secondly, the whole bread crumbs thing was *your* idea. And thirdly—"

"Thirdly, you smell?" interrupted Hansel.

"You are so immature!" yelled Gretel.

"At least I don't smell!" said Hansel.

While Hansel and Gretel were distracted, Wolfie crept silently away. He hoped the twins were going to be OK, but it was clear there was *no way* they would be able to work together right now. He was going to have to go it alone.

Everything was better now that Wolfie was free of the twins' constant arguing. He found that he could use his keen wolf nose to smell anyone that came near and hide in plenty of time. All the imps he saw were going in one direction, carrying fertilizer, water, and plant food, then coming back carrying nothing but empty wooden buckets. They had to be going to the Story Tree cutting!

After a while, Wolfie was *almost* beginning to enjoy himself. He felt daring, brave, and like some sort of secret agent. He crept through the wooden corridors, silent as the night, pretending to be on an incredibly dangerous and important mission. Then he remembered he *was* on a dangerous and important mission and got all nervous again.

He took a few deep breaths to calm himself and continued around the next corner.

"Hello," said the man from the looking glass. "Fancy seeing you here!"

"Eeeeaaarrrkkkk!" shrieked Wolfie, leaping backward.

"Oh, there's no need to worry!" said the reflection as a couple of sweaty imps heaved the empty mirror along behind him on the wooden cart. "After all, I can't *physically* harm you."

Wolfie breathed a sigh of relief and inched closer, trying to get past the reflection.

"However…" said the reflection, "I do have…my *underlings*!" He barked a command, and another group of nervous imps stepped out of a door behind him.

"Come on, guys!" said Wolfie to the scared imps. "I don't want to hurt anyone! Why don't you just let me go past?"

The imps looked at one another, then Wolfie, then the reflection, and finally down at the floor as they shuffled their feet and moved out of the way. "And you *really* shouldn't be working for him!" added Wolfie. "He's *not at all* nice!"

"You're pathetic!" roared the reflection at the imps. "Looks like I'd better do this the old-fashioned way!" His eyes flashed with a sickly green light, and the plants, branches, and roots of the palace began to snake around, rearranging themselves into a new shape. A round sort of shape. A big, "hole-y" kind of shape that was opening right beneath Wolfie's feet. He tried to step around it, but the hole opened faster and faster. There was no way he could avoid it.

"Yeaaarrrrghhhhh!" yelled Wolfie as he lost his footing completely and tumbled into blackness.

8
The Instruction Manual

"Urrrnnnngh..." groaned Wolfie. He was sprawled out on a soft floor surrounded by straw, moldy plants, and the unmistakable smell of rot. Flies buzzed, worms slithered, and unpleasant things crawled *everywhere*. Wolfie realized the awful truth: he was in a *huge compost heap*. "Eeeeuuuchhh!" he squealed, leaping up and wiping off as much of the stinking mess as possible.

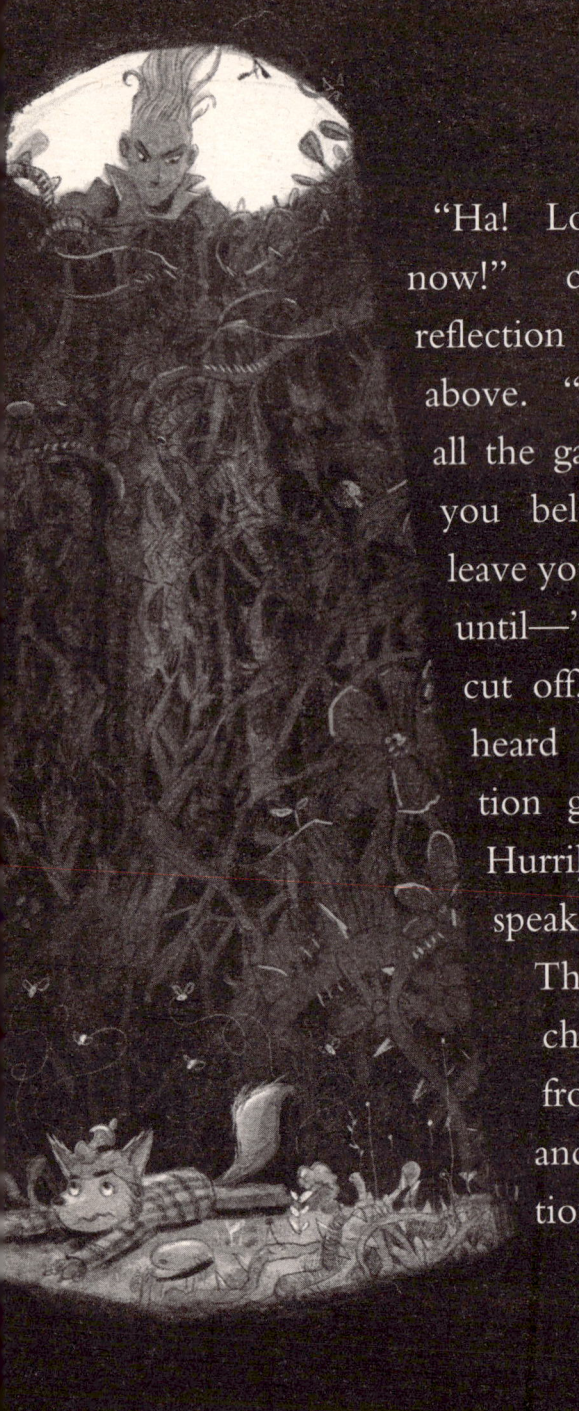

"Ha! Look at you now!" cackled the reflection from high above. "Down with all the garbage where you belong! I shall leave you down there until—" His voice cut off, and Wolfie heard the reflection gasp. "What? Hurrilan wants to speak to me now?"

There was a chattering reply from the imps, and the reflection called down to Wolfie, "Look, I've got some work to do, OK? I'll come back to continue taunting you in a little…"

"All right!" Wolfie yelled. "No rush."

"Thanks for being so understanding," the reflection called back.

Then there was silence.

Wolfie peered around in the gloom, hoping he might discover a way out. He explored every inch of the cavernous compost heap but found nothing. The walls were so slick with rotting compost juice that each time he tried to climb up, he slid right back down, squelching into the filthy muck. Things were not looking good. "Oh no, you don't!" he muttered

SNIFF! as he plucked a wood louse from his ear. A worm was perched on the top of his hat, an earwig was trying to wriggle up his nose, and his best necktie was ruined. All in all, it wasn't the best day he'd ever had. So Wolfie did the only thing he could think of: he sat down on the floor and cried.

"Don't worry!" came a gentle voice. "It's not so bad down here. Besides, there's plenty of food."

"Who's there?" asked Wolfie, his heart pounding.

"Only me," said a grubby-looking imp, poking his head out of the filth. "I got banished for breaking the magic mirror's favorite mirror. He's very vain, you know. '*That's seven years' bad luck for you,*' the mirror said as he threw me down here, then he laughed."

"That's *awful*!" said Wolfie.

"I know," replied the imp. "He makes some *really* lame jokes!"

"I was thinking more about being trapped down here for seven years."

"Oh yeah, right. That too!"

"So what about the food you mentioned?" asked Wolfie. "I am kind of hungry."

The imp grinned as he rummaged around in the filth and pulled out a juicy worm.

"Ohhh…" said Wolfie. "You know what? I've just remembered. I'm not *actually* hungry *at all*! Isn't that odd?"

The imp shrugged and popped the worm into its mouth, chewing away happily as Wolfie tried not to be sick.

"So…what's your name?" asked the imp, its mouth full of half-chewed worm.

"Wolfie."

"Hi, Wolfie, I'm Karpit."

"Seriously? Like, the things you put on the floors?"

Karpit shrugged. "Laugh all you want, but don't *ever* laugh at my uncle Dawmatte. He's got a black belt."

"What in? Karate? Judo?"

"No, on his pants!" said Karpit, looking confused. "Still, we'd have to escape from *here* before you could start offending my uncle!" He slumped down on a pile of rotting dandelions, which slipped to one side, leaving him sprawled out on the filthy floor.

"Typical!" muttered Karpit.

"Wait!" exclaimed Wolfie. "What's that…down where you were sitting? I can see something!"

Poking up out of the compost was the top of a book. Together they scratched at the dirt, digging away until Wolfie was able to pick it up and wipe it clean.

On the cover it had a picture of the magic looking glass and the words:

iMirror
User's Guide

"Whoa!" exclaimed Karpit. "What does it say?"

Wolfie opened the book and started reading. "'Congratulations on choosing iMirror. Most mirrors offer you a glimpse of the world around you. iMirror gives you the world you want…'" He paused. "It goes on like that forever!" Wolfie skipped through a lot of pages. "Wait! This sounds interesting. Listen… 'iMirror is manufactured to the highest standards, but if iMirror is left active for too long, it may develop personality "issues." If iMirror becomes "problematic" you may switch it off and return it for a full refund or simply break it using the enclosed magical hammer, bringing an end to any undesired magic. Please note your personal safety in either course of action is *not* guaranteed.' The magic mirror must have become faulty!" exclaimed Wolfie. Then his face fell.

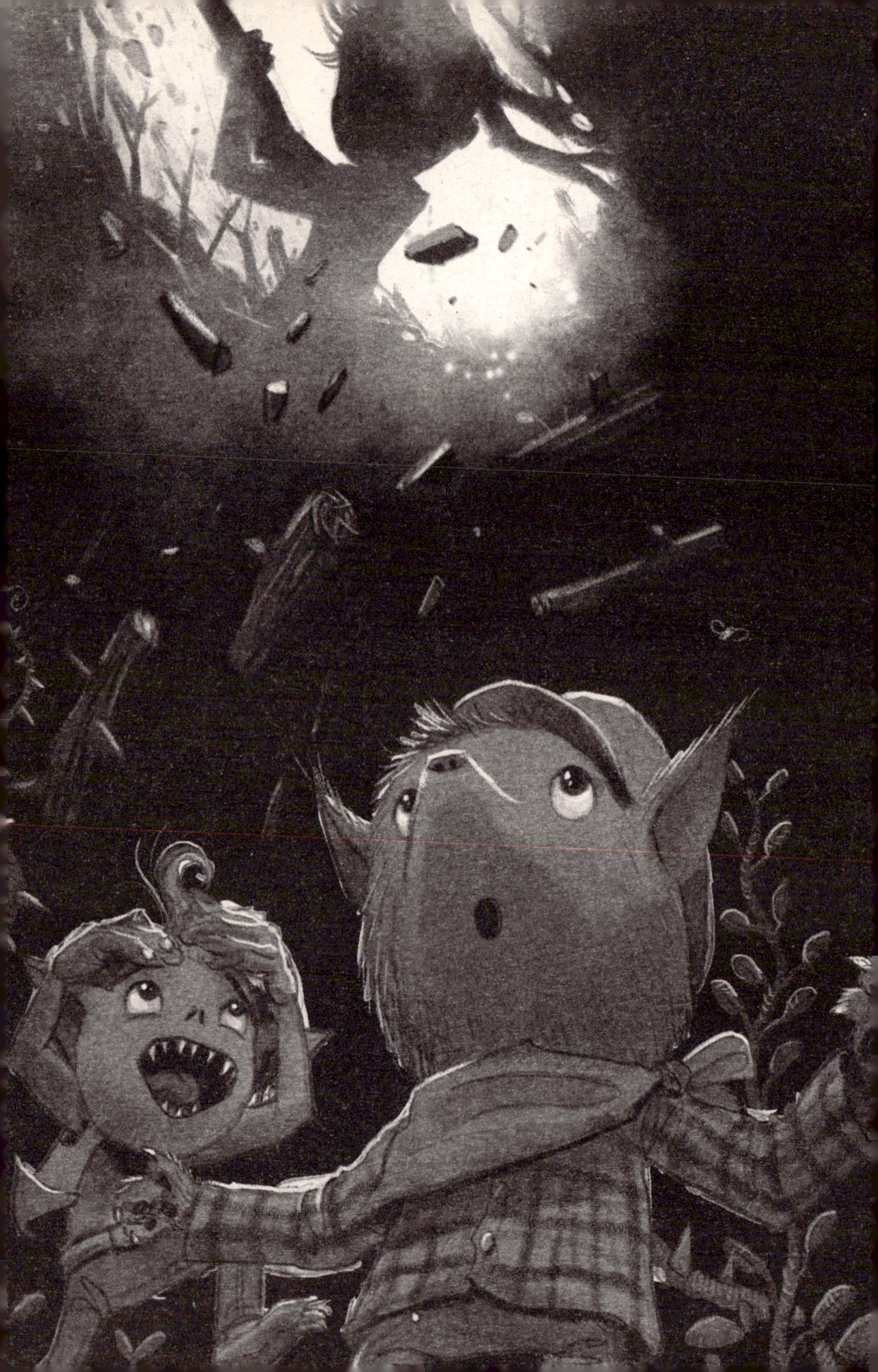

"But without that hammer we've got no chance of stopping it. We'd never get close enough to just turn it off!"

"Wait a minute!" cried Karpit. "I saw something like that the other day!" He started digging around, sending banana skins, carrot peelings, and less recognizable—but equally disgusting—things flying. "Now where was it...?" He dug on for a minute or two before holding a very dirty glass hammer in the air and shouting, "Aha!"

"Amazing!" exclaimed Wolfie. "Now we've got everything we need, except for a way out of here..."

There was a sharp chopping sound, and wood chips scattered down on top of them. A flare of light appeared about ten yards above their heads and a shadowy figure came into view.

"Oh no!" Wolfie cried. "He's back! Quick, pass me the hammer. I'll hide it!"

Karpit shoved the hammer into Wolfie's hand and dived beneath the top layer of compost. The end of a rope slapped onto the ground. Wolfie managed to tuck the hammer under his shirt just as someone landed right in front of him.

"Hey, Wolfie!" said Gretel. "Nice place you've got here!"

9
A Comedy of Errors

Gretel climbed back up the rope and heaved Wolfie through the hole she had hacked, but the branches were already weaving together. Wolfie only just managed to drag Karpit through too before the hole closed completely.

"I know how to do it!" gasped Wolfie as they crouched behind some ferns in one of the living palace's long corridors.

"Do what?" asked Gretel.

"Fix *everything*!" replied Wolfie. He held up the hammer Karpit had found. "We can destroy the magic mirror and get you and Hansel back to normal!"

Gretel growled at Hansel's name.

"Whatever!" exclaimed Wolfie. "What we need to do *now* is get to the branch. I *bet* the mirror won't be too far away!"

Gretel smiled. "I know where the branch is! I was following some imps up to the main tower when I heard the mirror drop you into that compost heap. So all we have to do is fight our way to the top of the tower—despite the *very* real chance of almost certain death—find the branch, and escape through a courtyard full of trolls."

"Now that you put it like that..." began Wolfie.

"I'm in!" cried Gretel.

"And me!" squeaked a trembling Karpit.

"OK then." Wolfie gulped, his whiskers trembling in terror. "Let's go."

Wolfie, Gretel, and Karpit soon arrived at the foot of a huge spiral staircase that twisted around the edge of a tall circular tower. They could see all the way to the top, hundreds of yards above.

"This is the main tower," whispered Gretel. She pointed at a group of imps parading around in mismatched and ill-fitting armor on the third floor. "But we're going to have to get past them."

"How?" asked Karpit.

"Using *this*!" replied Gretel, swinging a grappling hook on a rope through the air and throwing it a few levels above the imps so that it caught on a twisting handrail. "Quick, while they're not looking!"

Wolfie and Karpit clambered onto the rope behind her.

Unfortunately, it turned out that Wolfie and Karpit were *not* good at rope climbing.

"My hands hurt!" complained Karpit.

"Hurry up!" whispered Gretel.

"*You* try climbing a rope with *paws*!" muttered Wolfie. "You have no idea how hard this is without thumbs!"

"Shh!" hissed Gretel.

A surprised-looking imp peered over the handrail. With a nasty grin, it pulled out a jagged dagger and started sawing away at the rope.

Gretel groaned and hooked her candy-cane staff into the wall. "Grab my legs!" she yelled as the last threads of the rope gave way, leaving Karpit clinging onto Wolfie's back while he dangled from Gretel's feet.

"*This* isn't easy with paws *either*!" yelped Wolfie.

"Hold on!" shouted Gretel, rocking her body back and forth until Wolfie was swinging over the staircase.

"Let go on the next swing!" grunted Gretel through gritted teeth.

"I'm not sure..." began Wolfie, but Gretel kicked her legs so hard that his paws slipped, and he and Karpit landed in a heap on the stairs. Gretel took one more swing, then flung herself over the handrail, landing in a crouch, before springing up to climb the stairs two at a time.

As Wolfie got to his feet, he noticed a figure a couple of floors above—it was Hansel! If Hansel and Gretel found each other, then it was game over! He *had* to keep them apart! But how?

Wolfie didn't deal well with stress. It was like those granny-eating lessons at Wolf School where he *knew* the answers, but as soon as he was actually *asked*, his mind went blank, and he couldn't remember whether you were supposed to eat the granny *first* and *then* disguise yourself as an old lady or the other way around.

A great roar rose up below him, and Wolfie looked down to see trolls pouring into the tower and starting to run toward the stairs. Wolfie's mind raced, and *then* he had an idea...

"*Trolls!*" shouted Wolfie, pointing to the base of the tower.

"I'm on it!" yelled Gretel, skidding through the badly dressed imps on the third floor, who all scattered, whimpering about it not being their fault. Gretel picked up a big ax one of the imps had dropped and started running back downstairs toward the trolls.

"Let's go!" yelled Wolfie to Karpit as they raced past Gretel up the stairs.

"*Wolfie!*" cried Hansel, as Wolfie finally made it to the sixth floor. His eyes narrowed as he saw Karpit, and he pulled out his nunchucks.

"It's OK!" yelped Wolfie. "He's with me! We've got to get to the top of the tower—that's where the branch is. Come on!" Hansel looked puzzled but shrugged, and together they all ran up the staircase.

"Oh yeah, watch out for the cuddlers!" called Hansel as they raced along a narrow section of the staircase lined with big, bushy plants that had incredibly soft leaves and made a purring sound.

"Cuddlers?" asked Wolfie. Hansel poked his candy-cane staff at one of the plants. Two big bushy arms shot out and tightly cuddled the candy cane. The purring got even louder.

"They're not really dangerous," explained Hansel. "But it took me *forever* to get free after one of them grabbed hold of me!"

As they ran on, Wolfie peered down to see

Gretel hacking through the staircase with the ax. With a sudden crash, the bottom two floors—*and* the trolls—fell back down to the bottom of the tower.

"At least we're a good way above," thought Wolfie. "It'll take her forever to catch up!"

Just then, Gretel fired an arrow with a rope on it toward the floor they were on and started swiftly climbing up.

"Gah!" muttered Wolfie.

"What's down there?" asked Hansel, frowning.

"Nothing!" lied Wolfie, while he tried to figure out what to do. "Actually, it's *trolls*!" he said, surprised at how easy he was finding it to fib. "Hundreds of them! We've got to hide!" He shoved Hansel into a hollow tree trunk and whispered, "*Stay out of sight!*"

Wolfie's heart raced. Gretel was nearly up to their level... What now? He spotted a couple of cuddlers right next to where she was going to climb over the handrail. He knew that he *should* warn her, but then the twins would definitely see each other again—and *then* what? He kept quiet and stood just out of sight.

As soon as Gretel heaved herself over the railing, the cuddler scooped her up into a huge, warm hug that completely surrounded her.

"The trolls have gone!" Wolfie whispered to Hansel a moment later. "Let's go!" He grinned as they ran up the last few steps. They were so close!

It looked like everything was going to be all right! He'd *never* felt better.

Suddenly, a swarm of imps poured out of the door at the top of the staircase and came running toward them, roaring and waving a ragtag collection of weapons. The weapons were mostly held backward or upside down, but they were *still* weapons.

To make things even worse, Gretel came running up the stairs and spotted Hansel.

"*This ends NOW!*" she yelled, pulling out her bow and sending arrow after arrow whistling through the air. Hansel ducked as the arrows flew overhead and thunked into the wall. The imps stopped where they were, looking nervous. For a moment, nobody did anything. But then something strange happened to Wolfie. He *knew* what to do, and he *actually* felt as though he could do it. Time seemed to slow down as he watched Hansel and Gretel approach each other, their faces twisted in anger. Wolfie felt strangely calm. He *had* to rescue the branch. He *had* to destroy the mirror. Nothing else mattered.

He climbed up the arrows that were stuck into the wall as though they were rungs on a ladder. Then he leaped into the air, caught hold of a vine, and swung over the heads of the confused imps. He let go of the vine at full swing and flew through the open door into the room where the branch was.

He sprang up immediately, his senses alert and tingling. *There* was the branch from the Story Tree, floating in the air, suspended in a stream of powerful magic. Wolfie didn't stop to think. He reached out to grab it, but as he did so, everything else faded into darkness. It was only then he noticed the man from the magic looking glass in the shadows on the far side of the room, smiling horribly.

It had all been a trap.

10
Through the Looking Glass

Wolfie found himself alone in a strangely blank space. It was neither dark nor light, just empty. It was hard to tell if he was standing on something or floating in the air.

"Where am I?" asked Wolfie, but everything sounded strange, as though he was underwater.

"I suppose you're wondering where your precious branch is?" echoed the voice of the magic looking glass. "What you saw in that room was just a reflection, a copy. The *real* branch is hidden here—in a world of my own creation—beyond *anything* you could imagine."

"Oh, I don't know…" replied Wolfie. "I've got a pretty good imagination. Do you have any graybows?"

"Graybows?"

"Yeah, you know. Like a rainbow that's just gray, not different colors."

"Er...well, no. But I *could* make some. I *easily* could!"

"What about spider shoes?"

"You mean shoes for a spider?"

"No!" laughed Wolfie. "I mean shoes that have spider legs and can walk around by themselves. Pretty cool, right?"

"*No!*" came the mirror's voice. "*Not* cool. I'm not talking about any of that. I'm talking about a world of *terror*! A world of *dread*..."

Wolfie nodded. "Sorry...I talk too much when I'm nervous or worried or scared, and I just—"

The mirror interrupted him, sounding cross, "You're doing it again!"

"Sorry…"

"*Anyway*…" said the mirror loudly. "How about I offer you a chance to escape?" Wolfie nodded eagerly. "So it's agreed!" the mirror continued. "If you manage to overcome your worst fears, you may go free and take the stupid tree branch with you. And if you don't… then you will be trapped here—*forever*!"

Trees shot up out of the nothingness, and smoke poured into the blank space, creating a dark sky. Seconds later, Wolfie was standing trembling in a small clearing as the mirror's echoing laugh faded away in the cool night air.

Wolfie glanced around, his heart racing.

The reflection had said he would be trapped within a world of his worst fears, and Wolfie had many, *many* fears…

While he waited to be attacked by an army of giant zombie beetles with laser eyes and swords for legs, Wolfie noticed a movement in the bushes near him. He was surprised to see a little old lady hurrying along with a small basket over one arm. She didn't look *particularly* frightening… Although one old lady had once gotten *really*

angry when he accidentally splashed mud on her dress, so you never could tell.

Another bush rustled, and in the darkness, he saw his father, the Big Bad Wolf, creeping along behind the old lady. Wolfie's heart sank. He knew *exactly* how this was going to end! Then Wolfie saw something that gave him hope. There *he* was in the bushes too—*another* Wolfie, though it looked like a different version of him. *This* Wolfie looked as though he needed a good bath and hadn't ironed his clothes in *forever!* Still, as long as the scruffy Wolfie could get to the old lady before his dad, then *hopefully* she'd be able to get away.

Wolfie watched as Scruffy Wolfie crept up toward the old lady and tapped her on the arm.

"Do you need some help?" he said kindly. The old lady nodded. "You should be careful in these woods," said Scruffy Wolfie. "*Terrible* things can happen."

"Oh, I know!" replied the old lady. "I got lost, you see. Thank you for offering to help!"

"Think nothing of it!" replied Scruffy Wolfie. "It's my pleasure!" Something about the way he said this made Wolfie's nerves jangle, and the next second... Scruffy Wolfie leaped forward and gobbled the old lady up in one bite.

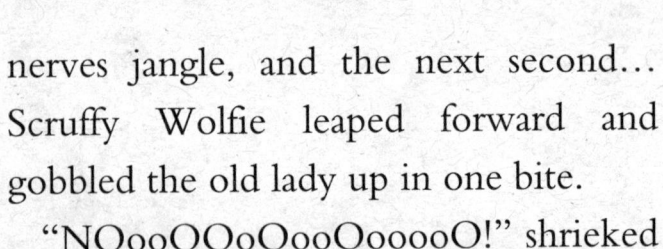

"NOooOOoOooOooooO!" shrieked Wolfie.

Scruffy Wolfie turned to face him and grinned horribly. "*This* is your greatest fear," he said. "You're a *wolf*! Deep down you know that it's true. You can't fight it forever."

Wolfie's heart pounded as the woodland scene melted away into nothing.

———◆———

For a while everything went dark again, then large oak trees sprouted up, and Wolfie found himself in a sun-dappled forest next to a path lined with pretty wild flowers. He frowned: *this* didn't seem very scary. Then he heard the sound of a girl singing softly to herself as she skipped along the path. There was a rustling in the bushes next to him, and his stomach churned as he saw a gray wolf-tail darting forward like a shark's fin.

"Look out!" yelled Wolfie to the girl. "*Run!*"

But the girl didn't seem to hear him.

Scruffy Wolfie emerged from the bushes and smiled at the girl as he leaned against a tree. "Your grandmother is ill in bed and has been asking for you," he said with a wicked grin. "Do hurry straight there!"

"Don't listen!" shouted Wolfie. "*It's a trap!*"

But it was no good. The girl thanked Scruffy Wolfie and ran off deep into the forest. Then the whole scene drifted away as though the trees were made of mist.

Moments later, Wolfie watched as an old wooden cottage built itself in the blankness next to him. Tall trees shot up around the edge of a small picket fence, and a brightly painted door swung shut. The scene was complete. He crept forward and peered in through the window to see Scruffy Wolfie lying in bed wearing a really, *really* unconvincing granny disguise.

"Seriously?" thought Wolfie. "That disguise is *terrible*! It's *totally* obvious that it's a wolf!"

His thoughts were interrupted by a knock at the door. It was the girl. Wolfie ran over and tried to block her path, but she just walked straight through him as though he wasn't even there.

"Wolves are wolves," sneered his father, appearing from nowhere behind Wolfie. "That's all there is to it! And *you* are a wolf."

"No!" shouted Wolfie. "I won't let this happen!"

"Too late," said the Big Bad Wolf. "It's happening *right now*…"

The scene shifted again, and now Wolfie was inside the house, right next to the bed where Scruffy Wolfie lay, pretending to be the girl's grandmother.

"My! What big slippers you have, Grandmother!" said the girl looking around the room at the scattered possessions.

"All the better to…er…keep my feet warm with?" said Scruffy Wolfie, then shook his head and roared. "Oh, who cares about all that rubbish! I'm *hungry*!" He leaped out of bed, ripping off his granny disguise—a nightmare vision of claws and fangs. The girl jumped back, screaming, and for a moment, Wolfie was paralyzed with fear. Everything seemed to move in slow motion as he watched the scruffy version of himself leap toward the terrified girl.

"No…" he whimpered,

feeling disgusted by how pathetic he sounded.

"*No!*" he repeated more forcefully, anger rising up inside him.

"*NO!*" he yelled as he sprang toward the evil Wolfie.

His mind raced. It didn't *have* to be this way. He could be whoever he *wanted* to be. It doesn't matter what his father thought or how the people of Tale Town felt about wolves. *He* didn't need to be on *either* side. He just needed to be himself.

"I would *never* do that!" he yelled and then howled his loudest, most wolfish *howl* at the evil Wolfie and the Big Bad Wolf. They both tumbled backward into nothing as the bedroom dissolved

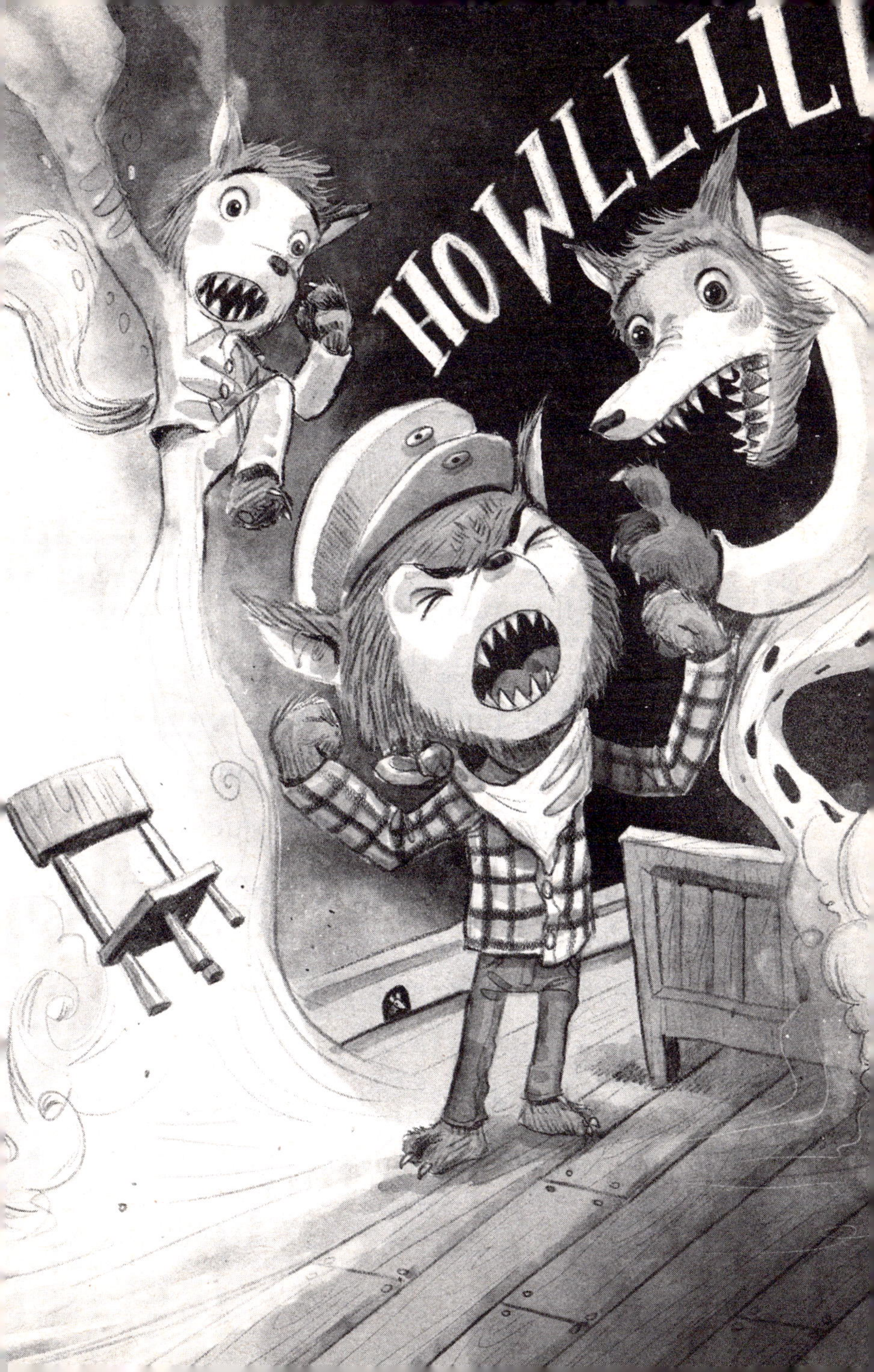
HOWLLLL

around him. This time the girl *did* see him. She smiled gratefully, and then she too disappeared.

Seconds later, Wolfie was back in the nowhere place with the branch from the Story Tree floating in front of him.

"No!" screamed the magic looking glass. "I don't understand! You should have been trapped *forever*! You should still be whimpering and screaming something like '*Help, noooo! The giant ants are drinking my brains with a curly straw!*' What went wrong? What did you see? What was your greatest fear?"

Wolfie grinned. "That I might be as bad as *you* are! But *nobody's* going to make me do *anything* that I don't want to!" He reached out and grabbed the branch. "So if you don't mind, I think *I'll* be taking this!"

II
The Dilemma

As soon as Wolfie grabbed the branch, he was transported back through the mirror's glassy surface and into the Green Man's palace. He looked around in confusion. Instead of being at the top of the tower, he was in the center of a large hall that was *filled* with terrifying statues like the ones in the courtyard. Hideous, ferocious animals and wild-looking men and women surrounded

Wolfie, their faces twisted in snarling rage. He watched as a sea of imps poured in from the doorway that led out to the tower.

Seconds later, the reflection burst out of the mirror and lunged toward Wolfie, passing straight through him.

"I can't believe that *you*, a pathetic, feeble excuse for a wolf, could have beaten *my* magical trap!" roared the reflection. Wolfie shrugged and was about to reply when he was distracted by a loud yell. He turned to see Hansel and Gretel burst into the room, still fighting bitterly. Behind them was a crowd of confused-looking trolls.

"*Stop it!*" yelled Wolfie. "I've got the branch! We can get out of here!"

"Great work, Wolfie!" shouted Hansel. "Just let me finish this off…"

"I don't *think* so!" yelled Gretel, swinging a huge branch at Hansel, who only just ducked in time. "Hold on! I won't be a minute, Wolfie!"

"Make them *stop!*" commanded Wolfie turning to face the reflection. "Put things back to normal."

"Or *what?*" asked the reflection.

"Or...*this!*" replied Wolfie, pulling out the glass hammer from under his shirt and waving it in the air. "Either you break the spell on them, or I break you *and* your magic!"

Wolfie wasn't sure what he'd been expecting. He'd never really done much negotiating before—unless it was to negotiate with one of his brothers by squealing, "*Please stop twisting my arm. It's really starting to hurt!*" Even so, he hadn't expected the reflection to laugh.

"Didn't you hear me?" added Wolfie. "This hammer will *destroy* you!"

"Yes, *yes*, I know!" chuckled the reflection. "I saw that you had it earlier. Why do you think I had the imps move the mirror to this hall?"

Wolfie frowned. "For a change of scenery?"

"Look around," said the reflection. "You see all these statues? You see how *wild* and *frightening* they look?"

Wolfie nodded.

"Well, all these statues will come *back to life* if you use that hammer. It was *me* that turned them into statues in the first place! Without my magic, you'll be at their mercy!" Again the mirror laughed. "So how about you give me back that branch, and I'll *think* about letting you and your friends leave in one piece. Deal?"

Wolfie looked at the terrifying beasts. There was one in particular that looked incredibly scary. It was a man with a beard made of thorny brambles that snaked through the air, the razor-sharp thorns glinting in the light. It was clear Wolfie would never survive if they were all freed. Perhaps if he made a run for it now, he could get out of here with the branch…but what about Hansel and Gretel? They'd be enemies for the rest of their lives, and it would be *his* fault. But if he returned the branch, there was no guarantee that the mirror man would keep his word.

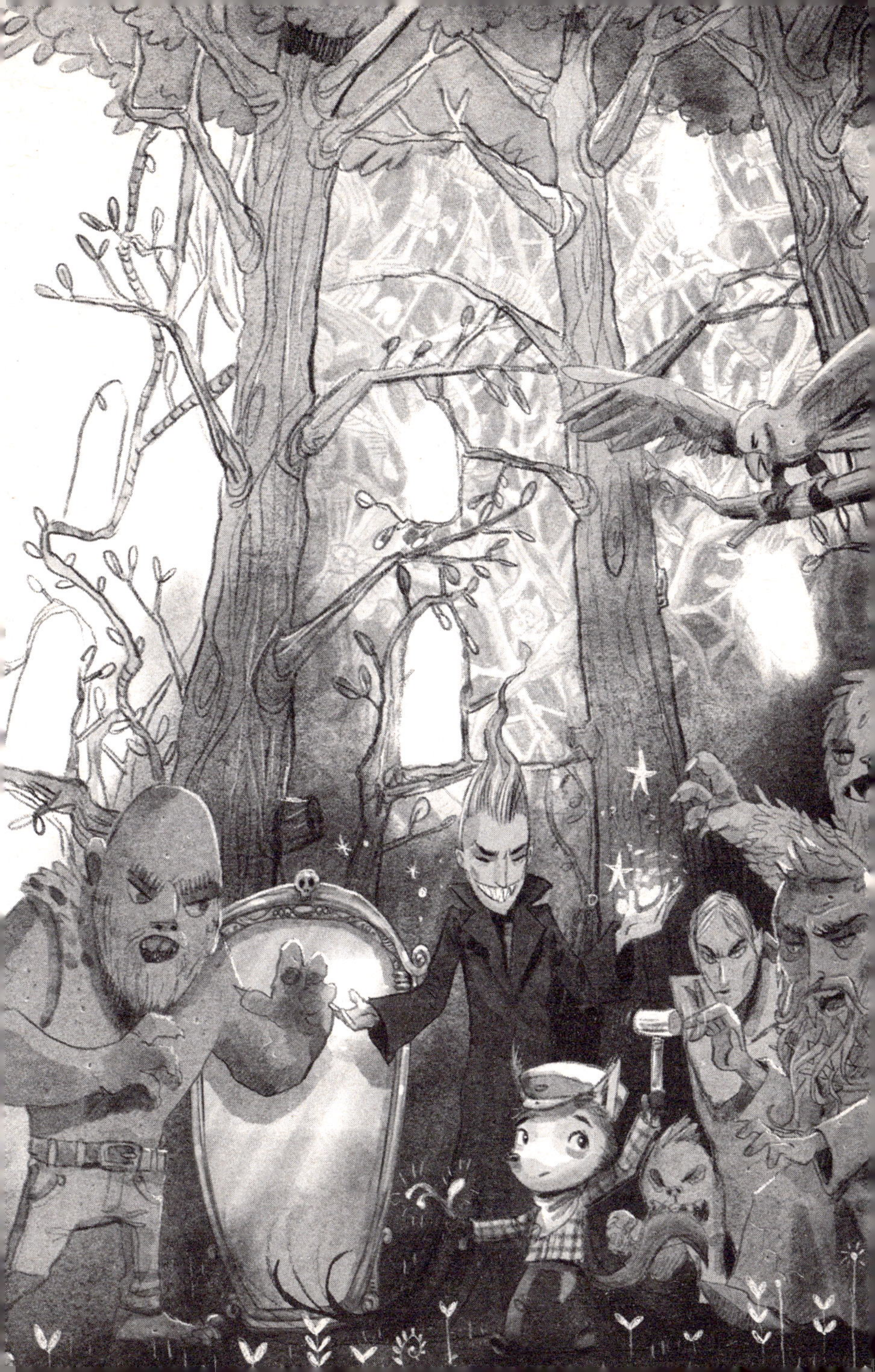

Wolfie took a deep breath and did the only thing that he could. He hurled the branch at Hansel and Gretel. "Catch!" he yelled as he dived toward the looking glass and swung the glass hammer forward as hard as he could.

12
The Awakening

Tiny shards of multicolored glass spun through the air as the magic looking glass shattered. Glittering splinters scattered across the floor, along with a pair of shiny silver shears, which Wolfie lunged toward and grabbed. For a moment, the reflection stood in the middle of the hall, looking shocked, angry, and scared, then it too broke into millions of pieces, which blew away on a howling wind.

Wolfie braced himself as the entire hall shook with the power of the released magic. There was a sound like a frozen lake thawing, a rushing creak that became a roar. First one, then another of the statues eased back into life, and seconds later, Wolfie stood in the middle of a seething mass of furious wild animals and monsters. He tried to bravely accept his fate, but

Wolfie was *terrified*. The last thing he saw was Hansel and Gretel's panicked faces as the army of creatures closed in around him.

"*Stop!*" rang out a voice with a deep woody echo. "*All of you!*" Wolfie peered out through one half-closed eye as the creatures fell silent. "We have been rescued! The looking glass is gone!" continued the tall figure with the thorny beard as he knelt down by Wolfie. "And I believe it is *this* brave young wolf who has saved us!" As he spoke, the brambles and thorns in his beard died away and were replaced with brightly colored flowers and ivy.

"So you're not going to do anything horrible to me?" asked Wolfie.

The tall man with the floral hair and beard smiled. "Not at all! When I discovered my magic looking glass had betrayed me, my friends and I tried to fight back, but the mirror cast a spell, turning us all into statues. I should imagine that we looked quite fearsome!"

"Kind of…" replied Wolfie, opening both eyes fully.

There was a sudden scuffle as Karpit ran over, wielding a rusty sword and waggling it around under the noses of the various animals and people. "You leave my friend alone!" the tiny imp yelled as loudly as he could.

The Green Man laughed kindly. "You're a very brave young imp! But don't worry. We're all safe now. The magic looking glass has been destroyed."

"And so has all of—"

"—*its* magic!" exclaimed Hansel and Gretel as they ran over, safely carrying the branch from the Story Tree.

"Well done, Wolfie, you—"

"—*totally* saved the day!"

"Only one more thing to do!" said the Green Man. "We have some uninvited guests who have outstayed their welcome." He pointed through the doorway at a group of worried-looking trolls who were sneaking away.

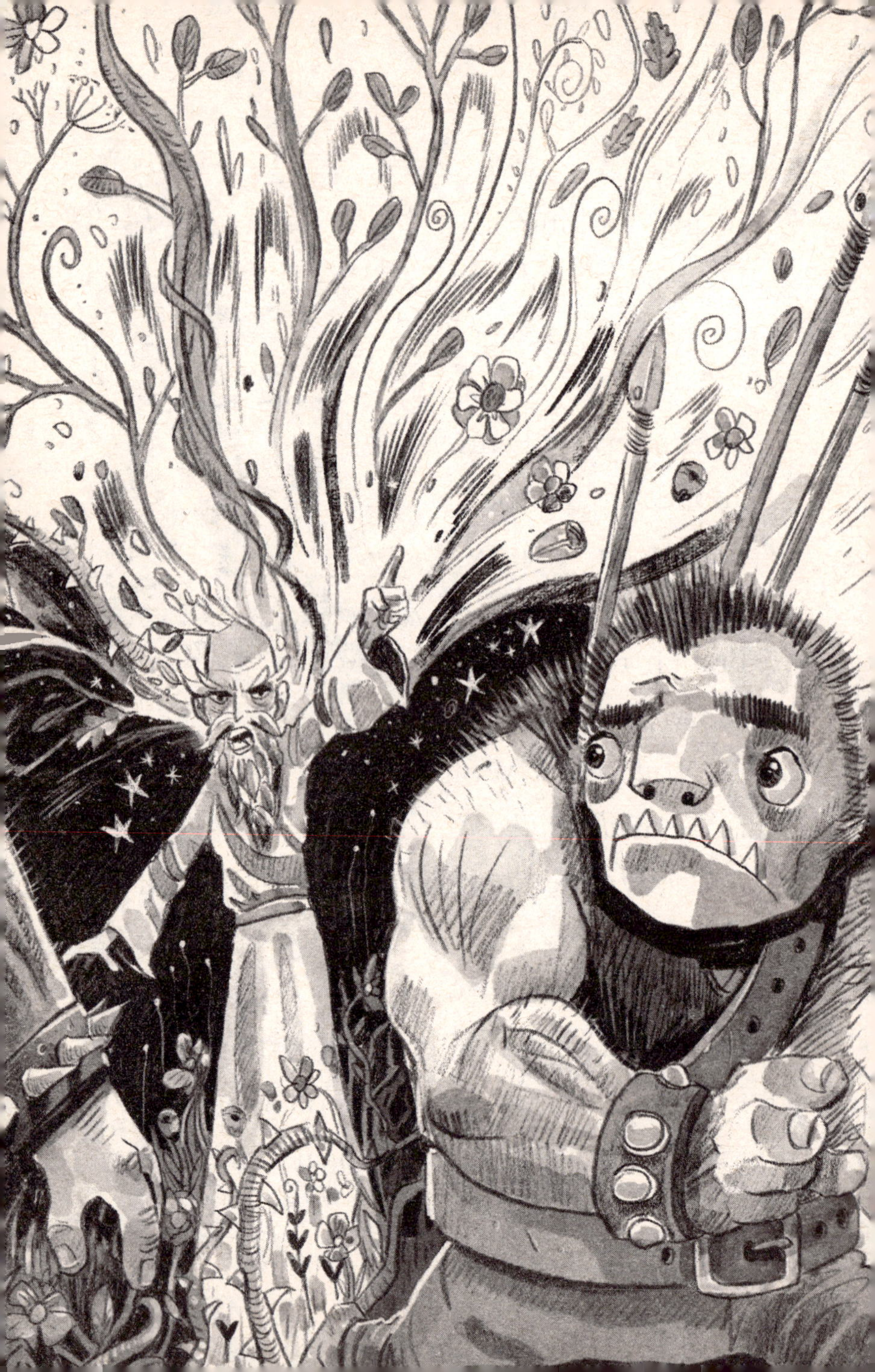

"I think it's time that our 'friends' left, don't you?"

The assorted pack of wild animals roared in agreement and raced out of the room to help drive away the trolls.

"And you can tell Hurrilan," the Green Man bellowed out of the window at the scattering army, "that my magic is *not* his to use!"

Then he turned back to the rest of the imps, who were looking nervously at one another and slowly backing out of the hall. "Well, this place is going to need a lot of tidying up!" He smiled at Karpit. "Do you and your friends want to help? I'll pay you all the worms you can eat!"

With a relieved cheer, the imps set to work. Karpit waved

cheerfully over at Wolfie as he found a particularly fat, juicy worm and gobbled it up like spaghetti.

13
The Truth Comes Out

The journey back to Tale Town didn't take long, but then again, when you're sitting in the branches of a walking tree that can step over rivers in one stride, it doesn't take long to get *anywhere*.

"Can you really get *any* tree to do this?" Wolfie asked the Green Man.

"Pretty much," replied the Green Man. "You just have to ask nicely. Wait a minute—I think someone down there is trying to get our attention..." He peered down at a man on the ground who was waving a sword at them and shouting, "You can't leave your tree here! Besides, all strangers have to be assessed by *His Worthiness* before entering Tale Town."

"But we live here!" yelled Hansel and Gretel. "And who's '*His Worthiness*'?"

"The mayor, of course!" replied the guard. "But he's very busy, so you'll have to make an appointment."

"Trust me," said Gretel, holding up the Sacred Shiny Story-Snipping Shears. "He'll want to see *us* right away."

It wasn't long before Wolfie, the twins, and the Green Man were waiting in the mayor's office.

The guard instructed them to sit quietly, to not touch anything, and to basically pretend that they weren't there, then left the room.

"What do you think of that creepy picture?" asked Hansel, pointing at a painting of someone who must have been Mayor Fitch's great-great-great-great-great-grandfather.

"Nice wig," said Gretel. "I might get

one like that!" She stood in front of the painting so it looked like the curly white wig was perched on her own head. Hansel laughed as he playfully shoved Gretel out of the way so he could have a turn, but as he did, she fell against the picture frame, which tilted to one side. Suddenly, there was a deep rumbling as a bookcase behind them swung open like a door.

Hansel and Gretel looked guiltily at each other. Wolfie's eyes widened, and the Green Man shook his head with a smile.

"*Whoops!*" muttered Gretel as she peered through the doorway. It led into a dusty cupboard that was empty except for a large stone with text carved into it.

"Hey, look!" she whispered. "This is

where Mayor Fitch keeps the 'Live Long the Story Tree' poem."

"Wait a minute…" said Hansel. They all peered closely at the stone, and Gretel gasped.

"The poem's different!" she cried. "The poem we know goes like this:"

LONG AGO, UPON THIS SPOT THE STORY TREE WAS BORN,

AND WITH IT GREW UP TALE TOWN, A ROSE WITHOUT A THORN.

BEWARE THE SHADOWS LURKING IN THE DARKNESS OF THE NIGHT,

WHO WANT TO TAKE AWAY THIS GIFT AND HIDE FROM US ITS LIGHT.

FOR IF THIS TREE IS DAMAGED THEN EXPECT THE UNEXPECTED,

THE STORY TREE IS SACRED AND MUST ALWAYS BE PROTECTED.

LIVE LONG THE STORY TREE!

"But listen to what it says on *this* stone—it's the rest of the poem!"

> **LIVE LONG THE STORY TREE! A TREE THAT'S LIKE NO OTHER.**
>
> **A TREE THAT COULD REPAIR THE WORLD, TURN ENEMIES TO BROTHERS.**
>
> **GROW STRONG THE STORY TREE! A TREE FOR ALL THINGS LIVING.**
>
> **FOR STORIES SHOULD BE FREELY SHARED. THE GIFT IS IN THE GIVING.**

For a moment, everyone was silent. "That changes the poem *completely*!"

Hansel cried. "*Someone* must have broken the stone in half. The Story Tree is meant to be shared with everyone—and Mayor Fitch knows it! He's been keeping this a secret!"

They were distracted by the sound of footsteps in the hallway. They rushed back to their seats, and Hansel tilted the picture straight again. The book case rumbled shut just as the doorway opened, and the mayor walked in. "What was that noise?" he asked.

"That was me—*sorry!*" said the Green Man, waving his hand back and forth in the air.

"I see…" said Mayor Fitch, his nose crinkling in disgust. Then he remembered what he was doing and put on his biggest, most charming smile. "I hear that you have news about our Sacred Shiny Story-Snipping Shears?"

"Not just news!" replied Hansel with a grin as Gretel pulled the shears out and handed them to the mayor.

"Well done!" enthused Mayor Fitch, his eyes lighting up greedily. "You have done Tale Town a great service. The names Handel, Greta, and Wolfo will be remembered as heroes!"

"Those aren't our

names…" said Wolfie, but the mayor just smiled and continued.

"What a treat to see such a well-trained wolf! One who seeks to *help* humans—to *serve* them. It is indeed a proud day!"

"Well, I wasn't exactly *serving*..." said Wolfie, but again the mayor ignored him.

"Did you manage to reclaim the branch that the trolls stole too?" he asked, his eyes flashing keenly.

"I'm afraid not," said the Green Man, giving a secret wink to Hansel, Gretel, and Wolfie. "The trolls were unable to use my magic properly, and the branch withered and died."

"Oh, that *is* a shame..." said the mayor, looking as regretful as he could. "Still, at least it's not in the hands of the trolls, eh? After all, the poem does say that the Story Tree *must* be protected!"

"Yes," agreed Hansel and Gretel. "We *all* know the poem."

"Anyway, I'm sure you have lots of *very* important things to do..." said the mayor. "You now have my permission to enter Tale Town." He shook hands with the Green Man and Wolfie then wiped his hand on his trousers when he thought no one was looking.

"Thanks again!" he called, his smile falling from his face as soon as they had left the room. "My guards will escort you out!"

As they left the Town Hall, Hansel turned to the Green Man. "That was quick thinking to lie about the branch!" he whispered.

"Well, I'm not entirely sure that your friend Mr. Fitch can be trusted," replied the Green Man. "I think perhaps it's a good idea for *you* to keep the branch safe for now."

14
The Secret Garden

Although Tale Town was still on troll alert, Mayor Fitch had finally found someone to blame for breaking the Moonstone defenses. Apparently it had been someone's Fairy Godmother (or Godbrother or Godsister or Godniece), and the mayor and his guards were busy tracking down as many fairies as they could to try to figure out exactly who was responsible.

People were once again allowed to move around Tale Town as they pleased, so Hansel and Gretel called for a *top secret* meeting with their friends later that day.

"What's going on?" asked Anansi as soon as he saw the twins, his eyes bright with excitement.

"I'm so glad you're OK!" cried Red.

"What happened?" asked Jack.

"Whaaat?!" squawked Betsy.

"Sorry, Betsy!" Gretel laughed. "We didn't get you a present, but we *do* have an *incredible* story to tell."

"But we need to go somewhere *really* private first…" said Hansel. "Come on. Let's go to the beach."

Between them, the twins, Wolfie, and the Green Man explained the whole amazing story. Anansi clapped Wolfie on the back when he heard how Wolfie had risked his life to save the twins. Jack and Red gasped when they learned about the secret second half to the Story Tree poem, and *everybody* had been astonished to see a tiny silver shoot sprout out of the branch that held *all* the details of their recent adventure.

The only person who hadn't really

warmed to Wolfie was Betsy. She kept looking sideways at him with her beady little eyes and muttering *"Whaaaaaat..."* under her breath.

"What's up, Betsy?" asked Red and jumped as Betsy clucked a *very* loud, *very* threatening *"WHAaAaaaAaaat?"*

"Oh, *come on*, Betsy!" Jack said with a laugh. "So what if he's the Big Bad Wolf's son? That whole business with Red's granny was probably just a big misunderstanding—right, Wolfie?"

"Um..." Wolfie blushed. "Well, not exactly..." He noticed that Red was looking a little nervous. "But that's my *dad*," he added firmly. "I'm *me*! And I can *promise* you that I'd never do *anything* like that. Besides," he added, pulling out a little bag of nuts, "I'm a vegetarian. So what are we going to do with this tree branch then?"

"I've got an idea…" said Red, looking relieved. "How about we pay our sea witch friend Lily a visit?"

"I'm *sooooo* hyped to see you guys!" exclaimed Lily as she flicked her fishtail to swim around her cave, deep under the sea. Wolfie was looking around in wonder as a school of fish drifted past him. It was Lily's magic that had brought them all down under the sea, and *somehow* that same magic meant that you didn't do anything horrible like drown either—though as Lily was only an apprentice sea witch, her magic didn't last for very long.

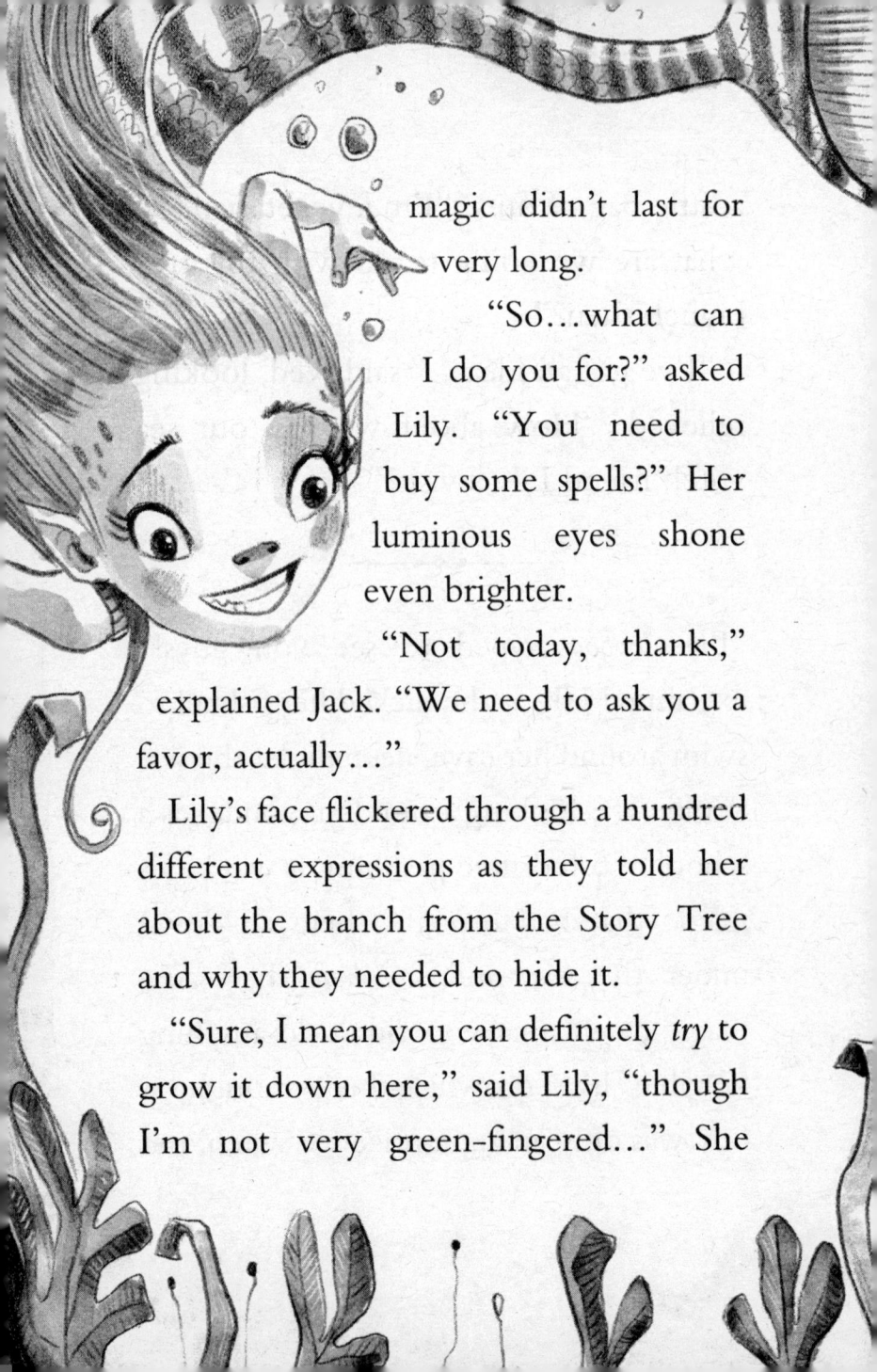

"So…what can I do you for?" asked Lily. "You need to buy some spells?" Her luminous eyes shone even brighter.

"Not today, thanks," explained Jack. "We need to ask you a favor, actually…"

Lily's face flickered through a hundred different expressions as they told her about the branch from the Story Tree and why they needed to hide it.

"Sure, I mean you can definitely *try* to grow it down here," said Lily, "though I'm not very green-fingered…" She looked at her green-tinted webbed fingers and sighed. "You know what I mean? I'm not very good with plants!"

"It doesn't matter!" explained the Green Man. "I can put a spell on the branch so that it will grow here, regardless of what you do to it! Besides, it's not like you can forget to water it!"

Together, Lily and the Green Man cast a spell to transport a small section of the woods from just outside Red's garden down into Lily's cave in a huge bubble, which he placed in the middle of a bright beam of sunlight.

"That should do nicely!" he said as he planted the branch inside the bubble. "I'll check in every now and then," he added, "but you shouldn't have any problems."

"*Awesome!*" exclaimed Lily breathlessly. "An underwater tree! I've always wanted to try climbing a tree! And riding a bike! *And* trampolining. Any of you guys got an old trampoline you don't want?" Everybody shook their heads. "Well, you'd better head home now! My magic's about to run out, and then it would be 'drowny-wowny' time!" She laughed brightly and waved good-bye as the whirlpool that had brought them down to her cave carried them all back up to the surface.

"See you soon!" she called out through the rushing bubbles. "*Adiós! Au revoir! Auf wiedersehen…*"

And that was it. It was done: the branch from the Story Tree was safe. Wolfie and the Green Man were taken to see *all* the amazing things that Tale Town had to offer—including Greentop's Cafe, where you could eat happiness-flavored toast; the market stall where you could buy a (temporary) flying potion; and the brand-new X-TREME petting zoo, with its baby dragons, griffins, and a phoenix.

Wolfie looked around at his new friends and smiled. He'd never really felt like he fitted in anywhere. But now—for the first time ever—he felt like he'd come home.

The End

Hansel

Strengths: Climbing, jumping, sneaking, and pouncing—basically anything ninja-like.

Weaknesses: Playing the violin.

Likes: His twin sister, Gretel; nunchucks; and gingerbread.

Dislikes: Broccoli and any other vegetable that looks like a miniature tree.

Wolfie

Strengths: Empathy, understanding, caring, and thoughtfulness.

Weaknesses: Well, for a wolf, most of the things listed above aren't super useful.

Likes: Blow-drying his hair and coconut shampoo.

Dislikes: Being mean, rude, or aggressive. Can't we all just get along?

Gretel

Strengths: Running, leaping, springing, and balancing—basically, anything ninja-like.

Weaknesses: Playing the tuba.

Likes: Her twin brother, Hansel; candy-cane weapons; and gingerbread.

Dislikes: Evil magic mirrors and being bored.

Hurrilan

Strengths: ALL types of troll magic and a commanding presence.

Weaknesses: His anger often clouds his judgment.

Likes: Smoky goat-flavored chips.

Dislikes: The way Tale Town people keep the Story Tree to themselves.

About the Author

Tom Percival grew up in a remote and beautiful part of south Shropshire. It was so remote that he lived in a small trailer without electricity or any sensible form of heating. He thinks he's probably one of the few people his age to have learned to read by the light from a gas lamp.

Having established a career as a picture book author and illustrator, The Little Legends is Tom's first chapter book series for young readers. The idea for Little Legends was developed by Tom with Made in Me, a digital studio exploring new ways for technology and storytelling to inspire the next generation.